MARGIE AND THE WILD DOGS MEET THE BIBLE SHREDDER

JOHN MURRAY

ISBN: 978-1-70-695119-3

CONTENTS

PROLOGUE

Once upon a time in a galaxy far, far away, there lived a young girl named Margie, along with her band of merry friends—Luke, Jose, Skittles, and Travon. They were known as "Margie and the Wild Dogs." They journeyed into another dimension—a dimension of sound, a dimension of sight, a dimension of mind, of shadow and substance, of things and ideas. It was there that they encountered the Bible Shredder. These are their adventures from beyond the Golden Wall. Their mission: to explore within its boundaries, to seek out Truth, Justice, and the Only Way, and to boldly go where no traveler has gone before.

This Sunday morning would be no different from any other for Margie. She woke up and got out of bed, brushed her long beautiful mahogany hair, then made her way downstairs. While enjoying her all-time favorite breakfast treat of graham crackers, she noticed she was late. Margie grabbed a few more crackers from the box and made it out the door within seconds.

The guard dogs protecting her home, or as she liked to refer to it as her "Castle," were four of the most ferocious and deadliest Doberman pinschers, trained for one purpose only—to kill on command.

Her father Biff was the president of the notorious motorcycle club, the Rips. He was the angriest and meanest biker in the club. But when it came to Margie (his little princess) and his wife Peggy, Biff's affection had no boundaries.

Margie held a special place in his heart, being his only daughter. Biff and Peggy also had two older twins. The twins, Dave and Duncan, handled their dad's bidding for the gang's daily criminal activity.

When Biff and Peggy had met many years earlier, Peggy was a motorcycle chick who went by the name of Poison. But when the twins and Margie were born, Poison dropped her rowdy self-absorbed personality and evolved into a sweet, gentle, loving mother.

Margie was only a few feet from the compound exit as she walked slowly and deliberately in silence, trying to slip away undetected before the Dobermans spotted her. With blistering speed, the dogs bolted straight toward her. It was too late for Margie as she let out a loud scream, begging the Dobermans to halt! At the same time, the four beasts at once pounded viciously on top of Margie's body, pelting her to the ground. They were licking, nudging, and rubbing their heads onto her face and body. She was laughing hysterically, begging them to stop.

Once able to calm them down, she walked them over to the pigeon coop that contained their dog food. Her dad Biff had been an avid pigeon lover since childhood; his pigeon coop not only housed hundreds of pigeons and dog food, but also his motorcycle and four-wheeler dirt bike. But Biff's love of pigeons was limited to homing and racing pigeons. He would buy tumbler pigeons by the dozens for the sole purpose and amusement of shooting them out of the sky. As those beautiful birds performed their natural ability of tumbling high in the sky, he would blow them to smithereens with his .22-caliber rifle. That weapon was his most prized possession; it was given to him by his dad for his thirteenth birthday. Sadly, only one week later, Biff's father would succumb to suicide over alcohol addiction.

After laying down several pounds of food for her precious

canines, Margie was able to escape the Castle. Margie and the Wild Dogs had some of the most exciting and carefree times imaginable. And that, my friend, is where today's adventures begin, so follow along and enjoy a day with Margie and the Wild Dogs.

1

A DAY IN THE LIFE OF MARGIE

The church building was only two blocks away from Margie's Castle, and as a Sunday ritual, she would skip past the House of Holies with a smirk on her face, defying her parents' instructions. Margie figured if church wasn't good enough for her mom and dad, it wasn't good enough for her.

Although Margie was below normal height for her age, she made up for it in her running ability. Lucas lived five blocks from the church, and as was typical, Margie's stopwatch would read between twenty and thirty seconds after her five-block sprint—once again, confirming in her mind that she would one day be an Olympic runner. Margie and Lucas had been friends since kindergarten, and as a tradition, she would hop over Lucas' white picket fence, then make her way up the cobblestone walkway to his front door.

"Come on, Lucas! Hurry up!" Margie shouted.

After a few knocks to the door and rings on the doorbell, Lucas answered. "I'm coming. I'm coming," he screamed with a protesting attitude.

Margie stood laughing in the doorway, watching his broad, husky shoulders droop, and with that slight German accent belt out the words, "I see nothing! I hear nothing! I know nothing!"—a reference to her favorite television character Sergeant Schultz from the television show Hogan's Heroes. Margie and Lucas had a special bond because on December 25th, only four months earlier, both had celebrated their thirteenth birthdays.

Sprinting two blocks together, they made their way to Travon's house. Travon had been part of the same kindergarten class as Margie and Lucas.

He spit out his toothpaste and held his eardrums while his mom belted a screeching holler from downstairs: "Margie and Lucas are at the back door!"

Travon made a quick zip down the stairs. He grabbed his bag of olives from the breakfast table while animating the bangs from the back door with air punches into the sky.

Upon seeing Margie, Travon immediately asked, "Did she see you?"

"No" was her reply as she winked at him, as if both had just pulled off a bank heist.

Travon's aunt was a nun at the church, and on most occasions, Margie walked on the opposite side of the street to avoid the obvious —that another Sunday they were all skipping church.

In disbelief, Lucas needled Travon: "What the heck happened to your Afro?"

What was once a lustrous and beautiful natural Afro was now a mini-Afro. His answer was that his mom had gotten into an argument with her boyfriend and had taken out her frustration on him.

The three were now all revved up and hurried to Skittles' house, hoping he would be ready and raring to go! Skittles had met up with Margie, Lucas, and Travon while in the first grade and quickly attached himself to the small cluster. The three of them were clowning around, leapfrogging over each other the final hundred feet to Skittles' door.

The chanting could be heard blocks away as they shouted up toward his bedroom window: "Skittle bum! Skittle bum! Skittle bum!"

That chant was the chorus line to a song Margie had made up

about Skittles years earlier. He poked his redheaded, freckled face from the bedroom window and gestured for them to catch him.

Travon yelled up to Skittles: "Just trust Jesus!" to which Skittles replied, "Don't need him—I'm Rocket Man!"

He jumped out of his second story window, and as his lanky body flew, it descended like a rock, crashing down on top of Margie, Lucas, and Travon. As they tried to break his fall, the momentum sent the group flopping and rolling on the grass. They could not speak because they were laughing so hard, but Margie managed to squeal out in a broken tone that she was about to wet her pants.

The last comrade to round out the gang would be Jose. But the task would not be an easy one. Jose lived alone in a shanty, or rather, a makeshift clubhouse outside of town in the woods. Jose's family had moved to town from Puerto Rico while Jose was yet a baby. He was quickly inducted into the Wild Dogs' merry band when they found out he called his father "Poppy." They liked the name so much that they called themselves "the Poppy Peasants," which lasted only until Jose's life-changing event. Jose was devastated when his parents died in a horrible car accident when he was only ten years old. From that moment on, the Poppy Peasants were referred to as "Margie and the Wild Dogs," a reference to Margie's Doberman pinschers always pounding her to the ground—out of respect to Jose. The town's authority tried placing Jose in several different foster homes but found he would continually run away. The town eventually adopted him as their own, but Jose was unaware of the special pact the town had with him. He would move his shanty from place to place in fear of the town's grown-ups. He believed that he would be sent back to a foster home.

The morning fog was still hovering over the woods, and it was so low they couldn't see five feet in front of them. As their walk turned into a slow crawl, they locked arms to avoid losing one another. Murky mud was below their feet, and they could hear the trees swaying from the brisk wind above.

Shouting out at the top of their lungs, "Jose! Jose!"—they could hear faint echoes shouting back the rhythm of their voices. After a twenty-minute search, they decided to leave the woods without him. Then they heard that famous Tarzan yodel coming from the treetops.

"Aaaaah-ah-ah-ah-aaaah-ah-ah-ah-aaaah!"

Down from the treetops came Jose, flying like a bird. He clung to a vine while leaping from branch to branch.

"Hey! Good morning!" he belched from a branch that only seconds later would crack, sending him hurtling to earth. As it snapped, Jose let out a loud "Yikes!"

With a crashing sound, he landed on a pile of leaves, sending them blasting into the air! His body lay twisted in the leaves, as grunts of pain and some Spanish curse words squeaked from his lips. He was now just a little torn-up jungle boy.

"Wow! That was fun!" he shouted while crawling to his knees.

"Where's the crowbar?" Margie asked him.

His reply was, "In the shanty."

She quivered, "Let's get it—we are wasting time!"

Even after walking through the woods and further from town with a cool, windy breeze against their backs for what seemed like forever, their attention couldn't be deflected.

There they stood like statues mesmerized, staring up at the twenty-foot Golden Wall. That wall towering over them encircled four acres of land, and they knew as adrenaline rushed through their young bodies that it was going to be a special day. The task at hand was to penetrate the wall and get inside. Lucas carried that huge, bulky crowbar with all its weight from the woods to their current location without a complaint. Although he liked to shell out orders and play practical jokes, this mission for him was a serious one.

Lucas' mom was known as "the bag lady" in town. She would talk to her dog Snoopy as if it were a fellow human being, following that beagle around with a brown paper bag. Onlookers would laugh as she would attempt to catch Snoopy's poop before it hit the ground.

His dad was a quiet, nonaggressive alcoholic who was always good to Margie and the Wild Dogs, shelling out a dollar here and a dollar there, saying, "Get yourself some ice cream! Make sure it's cherry vanilla—I love cherry vanilla!"

Lucas was also as stubborn as a mule and vowed he would get them onto the other side of that wall. Beyond the Golden Wall held the truth, as rumors filled the town with tales of secret kingdoms, space aliens, fantasies of utopia lands, and even a graveyard. These fables and others had swept through the town for years.

As sweat dripped from his forehead, Lucas squeezed the crowbar between two golden plates at the bottom of the wall, as he promised access into the most forbidden piece of private property the town had ever known.

He screamed in a loud and clear voice, "Mr. Gorbachev, tear down this wall!"

Margie and the rest of the Wild Dogs laughed as they watched the frustration bulging from his face with red veins popping out of his forehead. The two plates defied the jolts, wallops, and jerks as Lucas tried to break them apart.

"Hand it over! Hand it over!" said Skittles.

Skittles was a quiet teen but a risk-taker, and short-tempered. He was as eager about getting through that wall as any of them. Lucas, with little protest, surrendered the crowbar.

Skittles also had an alcoholic dad who drove a forklift in the town's apparel factory. One story Skittles often told about his dad that would bring side-aching laughter to everyone was when Mr. Skittles drove his forklift off the loading dock after having one too many beers. Skittles would mock and imitate his dad with hand gestures and summersaults, pretending to be his dad driving that lift off the dock.

His sisters, Mary and Elizabeth, had a singing group called the "Skittlets." They would perform cover band melodies in Lou's local diner on Saturday nights, as well as every Friday on the street corner, to crowds of enthusiastic onlookers. Skittles took hold of the large crowbar with both hands, using every ounce of his strength as he yanked at those plates. His yanking caused a tremendous *BOOM-BOOM* sound. The sound ricocheted off the gigantic Golden Wall, ripping into the teens' eardrums. As Skittles started to get his hearing back, he chuckled—then, he threw the crowbar onto the ground while laughing at the idea of impeding the metal plates.

Travon screeched, "Wimps! You're a bunch of wimps!"

Travon was an unconstrained buckaroo, causing havoc when given the opportunity. His nickname was Pits. This was because he would carry a bag of green olives, spitting the pits out at unsuspecting victims. Pits picked up the iron lever and challenged the mighty wall.

He screamed, "God, give me strength!"

Then, swinging it like a baseball bat, he landed a titanic blow. To his astonishment, the crowbar bounced off the wall. The bar flew out of his hands and sent everyone running in different directions, taking cover from the flying crowbar.

Jose, who had defied all odds as an orphan living in the shanty, was a special friend to everyone in town. His concerns about foster homes had no warrant to the townspeople. Jose let out a screech as the crowbar flew inches from his head and landed on the ground.

He picked up the cold, lifeless metal bar and threw it against the wall, hollering, "What the heck do we do now?"

The group then crouched in a huddle on the dirt floor, tossing about ideas on what to do next. Continue with their prized undertaking and dream of discovering the mystery behind the wall? Or, drag their wimpy, useless, and fruitless selves back to town, as losers? They concluded that the crowbar method wasn't working but feared any thought of giving up.

They began to walk around the wall, hoping to find another way to get in. Observing bushes with thistles and thorns hedged up against the next section of the wall, they thought that this may be a way of getting in. The plan was to stay close together and protect each other from the thorns. The bushes were stinging and stabbing as they were ducking and squatting, trying to evade contact with them.

Pits took a bold move and tried a fast-paced run, bolting from the line. As he ran through the weeds, a thorn bush grabbed hold of his back and ripped through his shirt and flesh. As they parted that section of the wall and into an open area, Pits removed his torn shirt.

A riveted, nasty scrape lined his left lower back to his right upper shoulder. Pits' bucking attitude was on full display for all to see as he cursed up a prayer storm, which included the words "Mary, Mother of God!"

Margie calmed Pits down with a few pleasantries about his bravery. Then, she and Skittles plucked the tiny thorns from his back. The others were preoccupied searching for another way into the forbidden zone.

When it became obvious that defeat was their destiny, Margie sarcastically said, "Why not just climb over the wall?"

She then went on and explained the technique on building a human ladder. Within minutes, the excitement built as they looked and sounded like circus clowns playing with building blocks as Lucas volunteered to become the anchor for their human ladder.

Skittles climbed up and stood on the top of Lucas' shoulders. Pits was then lifted by Margie and Jose onto the shoulders of Skittles. In agonizing pain, the boys shouted to Margie and Jose to "hurry up!" Jose made his way up the ladder, kicking and slapping all the way. Margie was the final piece of the ladder as all cried out in pain once again: "Hurry up!"

It was a shaky climb, but Margie scurried quickly up to the top. They were pressed tightly against the wall just before the human ladder began to shake. Margie was only a few inches from the top of the wall but couldn't reach, so Jose grabbed her by the ankles and lifted her the final few inches. Margie hadn't given any thought as to what she would do once she reached the top, but she struggled and finally made it. Seconds later, she was left dangling from the twenty-foot wall as the Wild Dogs' ladder collapsed, sending everyone except Margie straight to the ground. She could hear hysterical laughter and moaning from the Wild Dogs below but resisted herself from laughing, out of fear she would lose concentration and tumble to the earth.

So there Margie hung high in the air with her hands begging for relief, due to the mounting pressure her body placed on those little fingertips. As her legs and feet desperately crawled toward the top of the wall, she made it! Her feet and legs were now able to pull the rest of her body up to the top.

Once on top, she stretched out on the wall, looking like a flying Supergirl. As she lay on the wall top, she listened as the Wild Dogs cheered her on from below. It took a few minutes before her nerves settled down; she then turned her focus toward the opposite side to see what was beyond the wall. Perceiving the danger, Margie didn't want to move her body in fear of rocking herself right off the wall top.

Although she tingled with fear, the preoccupation of looking down at the landscape amazed her. She was a spectator, observing hundreds of gold tethered trucks littering the humongous lot. Many of the trucks were piled one on top of another—cranes, flatbeds, street sweepers, bulldozers, eighteen-wheelers, along with an army of discarded golden railroad ties.

Whispering from her breath, she said, "I will name this place the Golden Graveyard."

Now her task was to figure out how to get off the wall and down into the graveyard without killing herself. As her eyes searched back and forth, she believed her fate was to be stuck up there for hours. Determined to get down, she noticed two of the large flatbed trucks sandwiched one on top of the other, positioned just below her.

Her plan was to hang from the top, then drop down onto the truck closest to her. When she was finally about to make her move, she took a deep breath and whispered, "Yabba-dabba-doo!" as she shimmied her body off the top of the wall. She was now left dangling by her fingertips, looking for the courage to let go. After what seemed like an eternity hanging there, she regretted her decision and shimmied her way back up to the top. Retaking her Supergirl position, she was once again lying flat on her stomach on the top of that Golden Wall. Only, this time, she was frozen in fear and not able to look down or speak to the Wild Dogs.

2

THE TOMB

Meanwhile, below that immaculate wall, roaming around like zombies, the Wild Dogs pondered and regretted the decision that had placed Margie in such grave danger.

"Look at her," Skittles said. "She can't move, and one good strong breeze will blow her right off the top."

Margie was like a sister to the Wild Dogs, and their concerns were now larger than life.

Ideas were flying as Lucas thought calling the fire department might be a good idea. Jose came up with the brilliant idea of rebuilding the human ladder but then vetoed his own idea, remembering he had to lift Margie several inches to the top, and he believed he couldn't reenact it in reverse. The fire department idea was also rejected, in fear they would all be sent to prison.

Stuck up on the wall top, Margie quickly became their second concern as Pits saw a vicious black panther slowly heading in their direction. From the stare in the eyes of that hungry beast, they quickly became its prey. Grabbing sticks and stones to break its bones, the Wild Dogs began a full frontal assault onto the panther. Although they managed to bounce a few stones off its head, that only agitated it more. That big black cat continued picking up speed, and within seconds, it was leaping through the air, ready to pounce on them.

Crying in panic, Lucas—always one for a good joke—could be heard from under his breath, saying, "I only need to outrun one of these suckers!"

It looked now as if Skittles would be the panther's dinner. Just before that creature would pounce on Skittles, they heard a loud *BOOM*! With one shot, that black panther was dead, and there stood an old man wearing a cowboy hat, sporting a Santa Claus beard. The boys watched in awe as puffs of smoke continued to trickle from the shotgun barrel.

"Whoa!" said Skittles as he fell to his knees with praying hands, crying out with thanks to the old man who had just saved his life. Any notion Skittles previously had about God being a myth vanished.

As the old man stood before them, he was bombarded with questions. "Who are you?" "Where did you come from?"

They rambled on for a few minutes before the old man abruptly interrupted them. "Quiet! Quiet! My name is Gabriel, and I come from the same town as you. I have known all of you since you were born."

He looked at Skittles and said, "I am a big fan and watch your sisters Mary and Elizabeth perform at Lou's Diner every weekend. I also worked with your dad at the apparel factory."

"Really?" Skittles looked stunned.

"Yes, and I am sure you were never told the truth about your dad driving the forklift off the dock that day."

"Truth? What do you mean truth?" muttered Skittles.

"Your dad was not drunk that day—he was sober and saved a man's life with his heroic actions."

"What do you mean?" Skittles asked again.

"The drunk man that day was not your dad. It was Andy Schaffer. The forklift would not stop as Andy fell in front of it, and your dad's quick reaction saved his life. Instead of running over Andy's body, he took himself and that lift to a staggering five-foot journey, slamming it onto the pavement below the dock." Skittles' red freckled face now turned as white as a ghost, not believing his ears.

Gabriel continued, "Had your dad confessed the truth, Andy would have been fired. With eight children at home, Andy needed that job, so your dad took the blame. Skittles, your mom and dad are good people." Skittles' face regained its color, and with a sheepish smile, he nodded his head softly.

Then, Gabriel looked at Lucas and said, "I love Snoopy and vanilla ice cream." Lucas was stunned. Gabriel told him, "Lucas, your sense of humor is staggering, even in the midst of danger."

Pits then put his head down and looked toward the floor as Gabriel reached over and placed one hand onto his shoulder, the other outstretched hand made into a fist.

Gabriel said, "Travon, you have taken up my habit." Then, he opened his fist, and in his palm were five green olives. "These are for you, Pits."

As Pits took the olives, Jose started to walk away.

"Not so fast, Jose! Come back here," Gabriel said in a heartfelt voice.

Jose walked back with tears in his eyes. "I guess you knew my parents."

"I did," Gabriel answered. "I was there that tragic night."

Jose was now full of pain, as tears came pouring from his eyes. "Please tell me the truth, Mr. Gabriel."

"Yes, Jose, I will. It happened fast, and your parents endured no pain. The truck driver of that eighteen-wheeler fell asleep. He crossed over into your parents' lane before your dad could react. Your mom and dad loved you so much—they just wanted to get home to you that night. The driver of the truck that night was a good man who had driven all night trying to get home to see his dying wife. That man had several major breakdowns after that day, and today, he resides in the town's mental institution."

Then, feeling Jose's excruciating pain, Lucas, Pits, and Skittles gathered around him, giving a group hug.

As quickly as Gabriel had blown that panther from the sky, he was gone as the boys lifted their heads.

"Where did he go?" Those were the words for the moment, as their eyes searched the landscape around them. Both the panther and Gabriel had vanished without a trace. Skittles let out an eerie screech, then suggested after such an emotional roller coaster, that it would be best if they made their way home. All in agreement, they started a slow trek back to town.

Lucas then shouted, "Margie! Holy smackeroo! We forgot all about Margie!"

After their about-face, they began to discuss Margie's fate. "How are we going to get her down?"

"Rocks, we will use rocks," said Jose, "but we need to make sure she drops onto the other side."

"Rocks?" said Lucas

"Yeah, the fear will prompt her into action," Jose said. "Let's just make sure we don't unintentionally hit her."

Those ringing sounds coming off the side of the Golden Wall were the rocks targeting Margie, as were the screams from below, telling her to get off the wall and down onto the other side. Her only choices now were to take a chance on a ten-foot spiral onto a flatbed truck's rooftop and be on the inside of the Golden Graveyard—or a twenty-foot drop onto the ground below and be back where she started. As those stones flew past her head, she freaked and swooped back down to the graveyard side. Again, she found herself dangling with a ten-foot drop below. Her fingers felt as if they were being sawed off from the pressure of her own weight. After a few minutes of dangling, she couldn't take the pain any longer.

Margie let go and found herself flying with her arms stretched like a bird, trying to propel herself against gravity. Doomed for a crash landing, her body slammed onto the truck's rooftop below, then tumbled off the rooftop onto the flatbed. In a continuous motion, she rolled off the flatbed, crashing onto the ground. She was dazed and confused, and above her head appeared a halo of twinkling stars orbiting in circles. She was stunned from the blunt trauma.

Not seriously injured, Margie stood to her feet, and with a brisk sweep of her hands, she swept away those swirling stars from her eyes. If that wasn't enough for her to doubt her own eyesight, before her stood a four-foot rabbit wearing grim reaper garb, swinging a sickle, saying, *"Be strong and courageous. Do not be afraid or terrified because of them, for the LORD your God goes with you; he will never leave you nor forsake you."*

"I don't understand!" Margie murmured.

The rabbit spoke again, saying, "Your speed will be that of a rabbit, but your understanding as slow as a tortoise."

Then came a loud *ping, ping, PING!* The rabbit ricocheted like lightning from truck to truck, quickly disappearing over the wall.

Margie then detected rumbling voices coming from the other side of the wall: "Incoming crowbar! Incoming crowbar!"

Before she could make out the dialog, over the wall came that heavy metal baton, accompanied with a loud swishing sound. The crowbar landed on her foot, sending an excruciating pain up her leg.

She could hear the Wild Dogs screaming from the other side of the wall, panicking her into action. She stood up holding the crowbar in one hand, while massaging her leg with the other, then limped over to where the teens' voices were vibrating. Her task was to slam the golden panels loose with the crowbar from her side. She spent five minutes slamming, kicking, and pushing herself against those panels.

Margie was hitting them with such force that she became light-headed, then almost fainted. She was able to make a small opening to see onto their side. Then, Lucas told her to throw the crowbar back over the wall. As she looked up at the twenty-foot wall, she knew there was no way she would be able to throw the crowbar that high, but she gave several halfhearted attempts. Each time, she ran away to avoid having the crowbar landing on her head. Margie could hear the Wild Dogs banging away from their side, trying to make an opening wide enough to slip the crowbar through.

Success—they did it! The opening was now wide enough to receive the crowbar. Within minutes, they dismantled enough of the panels for entry. The opening was instantly crowded with young bodies, pushing and shoving their way into the Golden Graveyard. They were in awe that they were now on the inside of the town's most restricted area. Margie tried in vain to communicate her experience with the rabbit to the Wild Dogs, but each one took off running to the truck that most represented their fantasies from childhood.

Jose hopped onto a massive bulldozer, imagining himself pushing tons of earth into and filling a rapidly moving river, while Skittles slipped behind the controls of a large crane, envisioning himself sending large concrete slabs way up into the sky. Lucas jumped into the back of a garbage truck pretending to be a pig, snorting and squealing with laughter, while Pits was dancing the tango on top of a flatbed. Good times had just kicked in. Margie stood still as her nostrils noticed the smell of cotton candy. Between the rabbit and cotton candy, Margie was overwhelmed with an extremely uncomfortable feeling.

She shouted out to them in an alarming voice: "Get back here! Get back here!"

Without hesitation, each jumped from their selected truck and ran to Margie.

"Something is wrong! Terribly wrong!" she cried out.

The Wild Dogs looked at each other as if she had lost her mind; then, silence filled the air. Seconds later, the sky opened to mighty thunderclaps, while a rumble from below their feet caused a shift in the earth. The Golden Walls began to shake like rubber. Trucks began to unhinge as mechanical parts were zipping past their heads. It was a tremendous freakish earthquake.

Below them opened a sinkhole, sending Margie and the Wild Dogs into a free fall. The sweet smell of cotton candy that Margie had previously experienced was now everywhere. As they descended, ghostly figures appeared alongside them. What looked like a Cat in the Hat at one moment turned into a woman holding an umbrella floating through the air the next. Then, they heard loud bells and chimes coming from a red-nosed reindeer pulling a sled.

Along each side of them were long glass tubes; stuck within the tubes were princesses, princes, kings, and queens—all shackled in heavy metal chains crying out in agony and squashed one on top of another.

A mighty voice blasted from above as the words "Warp speed, Mr. Slinky," were heard, followed by "Yes, Captain."

Immediately, Margie and the Wild Dogs were falling faster than the speed of light. Then came heavy waves of warm thick air pushing up from below, which slowed them into a soft, gentle float.

That sweet smell of cotton candy began to dissipate as they landed onto a large colony of bunny rabbits. The group lay there motionless as hundreds of white rabbits hopped all over them. The little fuzz balls were everywhere, bumping and rubbing up against Margie and the Wild Dogs.

What now for the friends? Will they hop with the bunnies? Will the cottontails flip tails? Or will they stay ahead of the wabbit? Here they go!

After a few moments, Margie was able to stand, while bunnies jumped from her body and strip cloth and linen tangled her feet.

Looking around, she asked, "Where are we? What the heck just happened to us?"

In a quiet, bewildered mumble, Lucas answered, "I'm not sure, but it looks like an empty tomb."

"Empty tomb?" Margie said.

Then Lucas said, "There are carvings on the wall."

"What does it say?" Pits asked.

Lucas then began reading:

Early on the first day of the week, while it was still dark, Mary

Magdalene went to the tomb and saw that the stone had been removed from the entrance. So, she came running to Simon Peter, and the other disciple. The one Jesus loved, and said, "They have taken the Lord out of the tomb, and we don't know where they have put him!" So, Peter and the other disciple started for the tomb. Both were running, but the other disciple outran Peter and reached the tomb first. He bent over and looked in at the strips of linen lying there but did not go in. Then Simon Peter came along behind him and went straight into the tomb. He saw the strips of linen lying there, as well as the cloth that had been wrapped around Jesus' head. The cloth was still lying in its place, separate from the linen. Finally, the other disciple, who had reached the tomb first, also went inside. He saw and believed.

"Haven't we heard that somewhere before?" Margie asked as they moved toward the entrance of the tomb, trying not to squash any of the bunnies.

Lucas was about to answer Margie when the walls around them began to vibrate, and a voice spoke from the bricks, saying, "Hey Margie! Hey Margie!"

The words got louder and louder as Margie and the Wild Dogs started to tumble over one another. The herd of rabbits began tickling them into uncontrollable laughter. The laughter soon became doom and gloom as the walls opened, and out from behind them came three large super-duper Gillette double-edged swords. The razor-sharp blades began chopping each of their bodies and the bunnies into hundreds of pieces. The slicing caused them no pain.

As their blood flowed out from the tomb, it descended onto a white sandy beach. They were still conscious of their existence, although they were only blood. The bunny blood was separated from the human blood; the bunny blood evaporated immediately while the human blood splashed onto the shore.

As their red goo hit the sand, it immediately began clotting back together. Margie and the Wild Dogs could feel thick lines in the sand outlining their bodies. The thick lines then brought them back into a physical existence.

Margie was lying on her back in the sand, totally blown away from the experience. She then noticed the texture to be more like salt, not sand. She wiped her lips and tasted a salty flavor in her mouth. Rolling her eyes to the right, she saw Jose and Skittles, both buried up to their necks in sand. Margie lifted her body and moved toward them and began burrowing away. As she tried to unbury her friends, the small grains of rock disappeared with each scoop.

Then the words "Hey Margie! Hey Margie!" in a loud, high-pitched voice sent her to her knees. Then, *WHAM!* A title wave of water came crashing down, knocking her unconscious.

She woke up minutes later to slaps on her face, while hearing Jose and Skittles shouting, "Margie! Margie! Wake up!"

Quiet then filled the air as Margie slowly gained consciousness and her eyelids began to lift. Moments later, Margie, Jose, and Skittles found themselves sitting comfortably on the shore. They rested there as time slowly passed.

In a whisper, Margie asked her friends: "What's going on?"

Both cried out in laughter as Jose snickered, "Heck if we know! But it's been a nutty ride."

She said in a grimmer voice, "Come on—what's going on?"

"We don't know! We also have no clue where Lucas and Pits are!"

Margie burst into tears, crying like a wee little infant, assuming she would never again see her family.

Skittles lightly slapped Margie's cheeks to bring her back to reality while saying, "I'm not going to tell you everything will be okay, but everything will be okay!"

After pondering his most excellent wisdom, she began to calm down. She noticed a large battleship with colorful pegs sticking out from the portholes at sea. The floating vessel had already captivated the attention of Skittles and Jose.

"Do you see it?"

"Yes!" said Skittles. *Scream!*

Scream! "Help, help, help!" they yelled as loudly as possible.

Echoes from their voices could be heard for miles over land and sea. The words and sounds from their voices became silent as they watched Mr. Bubbles form next to the ship. Then, a large moving Yellow Brick Road broke out from the side of the ship. The walkway was heading their way as it jettisoned toward them.

The water divided into two halves as those deafening words "Hey Margie! Hey Margie!" once again returned—only this time, the high screeching pitch caused all three characters to fall flat on their faces.

They cried out in pain while cupping their hands over their ears. With the walkway now just feet from their heads, the sound faded. They slowly slid themselves onto the sturdy walkway flat on their bellies. The Yellow Brick Road then began to move in reverse back toward the ship. Jose and Skittles stood up and ran in the opposite direction as Margie watched a massive hole opening in the hull of the ship. A suction so heavy pulled her body toward the hole, paralyzing her from head to toe. Immediately, the hole slammed shut once Margie was inside.

She was captured and elevated by the tentacles of a gigantic octopus, then hurled to the deck, where she was momentarily pinned down, then set free. The octopus turned into an itsy-bitsy spider and went up the waterspout. As Margie stood up, animals appeared everywhere around her. The room became loud with elephants making trumpet sounds, ducks quacking, chimpanzees screaming, donkeys hee-hawing, hyenas laughing, pigs oinking, tigers roaring, and every other kind of living creature all singing in perfect harmony. That beautiful harmony was not by accident but by design. The designer was a maestro standing on the front deck and waving a little stick, conducting every sound those critters made. Margie had to make her way past large and small animals before she was able to reach and talk to the conductor.

As the maestro was taking his bow, Margie grabbed his baton, broke it over his head, and said, "Where am I? And what is going on?"

Stunned and with a surprised look on his face, the maestro said,

"My name is Noah, and I was instructed to load this ship with every kind of animal on earth."

Margie said, "I'm scared, alone, and haven't a clue what's happening to me."

"Calm down, Margie, and I'll explain."

Noah then went on to explain:

The LORD said to me, "Go into the ark, you and your whole family, because I have found you righteous in this generation. Take with you seven pairs of every kind of clean animal, a male and its mate, and one pair of every kind of unclean animal, a male and its mate, and also seven pairs of every kind of bird, male and female, to keep their various kinds alive throughout the earth. Seven days from now I will send rain on the earth for forty days and forty nights, and I will wipe from the face of the earth every living creature I have made." And I did all that the LORD commanded. And my entire family and I, entered the ark to escape the waters of the flood. Pairs of clean and unclean animals, of birds and of all creatures that move along the ground, male and female, came to me and entered the ark, as God had commanded me. Then the LORD shut us in.

He continued, "You, Margie, are the first outsider we have seen in months."

Margie sat there pondering her situation, then watched as Noah, his family, and the animals all turned into tiny bite-sized animal crackers, being gobbled down by a blue Cookie Monster.

Just then, the hole in the side of the ship reopened. Margie watched in horror as Jose and Skittles were launched through the air as their bodies slammed up against the bulkhead of the ship. Both were knocked out from the body bash. The impact released a large scroll stretching from the bulkhead to the deck.

The title on the scroll read "The Proverb Factory: *The Beginning of Knowledge.*" The following inscription hovered over the scroll:

These are the proverbs of Solomon, the son of David and king of Israel. They will help you learn to be wise, to accept correction, and to understand wise sayings. They will teach you to develop your mind in the right way. You will learn to do what is right and to be honest and fair. These proverbs will make even those without education smart. They will teach young people what they need to know and how to use what they have learned. Even the wise could become wiser by listening to these proverbs. They will gain understanding and learn to solve difficult problems.

The scroll stretched for miles as Margie had to crawl over what had now turned into an ocean of jumbo bean bags. She tried getting to her feet while flipping and flopping before reaching the boys.

Whispering in a tangible corky voice, she said, "Jose, Skittles—you okay?"

There was no answer from the lifeless bodies. Margie believed both to be dead, at the same time praying she was having a nightmare.

She heard faint music playing on the other side of the ship's bulkhead, then noticed raindrops in different colored configurations of dots, sliding down the interior main beam of the ship. Each dot started to squeak out individual words as it reached her face.

The first word squeezed was "Welcome," the second dot squeaked the word "Margie," the third was "to," and the fourth was "prince-area." As baffled and mystified as she was, she found it humorous. The dots continued rolling down the main beam, but only now, the dripping sounds were silent.

One of the larger pink dots dripped in slow motion and landed just next to her. The pink dot grew both in size and shape—it now looked like a pink basketball. Glancing down at the basketball, she saw two ruby red eyeballs pop out from the carcass of the leather ball, along with two dark purple lips. She continued looking down and saw the basketball staring back up at her.

Margie politely asked, "What is prince-area?"

In a soothing, tuneful voice, the nonbinary basketball said, "Follow me."

Margie looked back at Jose and Skittles, only to find them still in their dead man positions. Margie was then zapped with an overwhelming feeling of comfort and joy, so she followed the bouncing ball.

Without indication or warning, the interior wall lifted skyward, then disappeared into the ceiling. The basketball then bounced itself and Margie into a gigantic beautiful ballroom. Her eyes were fixed on the bouncing ball as she heard a symphony orchestra belting out many of her favorite tunes all at the same time.

How she was able to hear all of her favorite songs at one time and enjoy each separately was beyond her comprehension. The gorgeous ballroom was crowded with thousands of guests, sitting at long exotic tables. They had every kind of gourmet food the mind could conceive at their fingertips.

Beginning to accept her situation, Margie looked over at the basketball, hoping for some hint of what was going on. She watched the basketball deflate into a cranberry drink being sucked down by one of the guests. As the orchestra continued to perform and the guests continued to feast, Margie concluded that she was at some famous festival to honor a king or queen.

Margie walked around the room for miles while not a soul looked in her direction or spoke to her—it was as if she were invisible. With her favorite tunes still dancing in her mind, there was an underlying current below the music notes that sparked familiar voices.

Margie followed the voices, which she now recognized, and they pointed her to the main banquet table. There she found Jose, Skittles, Lucas, and Pits, all feasting like emperors. Not even one of them looked up from the buffet to realize she was standing there facing them.

Margie yelled at the top of her lungs: "You slobbering pigs!"

Now, she had their attention. They looked up at her with food hanging from their mouths and bloated cheeks.

She screamed out, "Where are we, and what's going on?"

Pits' answer was gentle and direct as he just looked at her and said, "Heaven—we are in Heaven."

"Huh? How? Heaven?" she answered. "I don't remember dying, and I sure don't feel dead."

Pits answered her: "Margie, please don't ask questions; just believe it! You are in Heaven!"

"If I'm in Heaven, I should be able to fly."

Immediately, she jumped onto the banquet table, only now she was wearing a Supergirl outfit with a big S in the middle of her chest. Margie kicked off the golden silverware and gourmet food from the table as Skittles and Jose ran toward her, hoping to pull her from the most embarrassing moment of her life. But before they could reach her, Margie began sprinting quickly down the lengthy table.

She was now in full throttle, moving faster than a speeding bullet. To her surprise, the hundreds of guests who were in the area still went about their business, as if she and the Wild Dogs didn't exist. Her moment had come, and the end of the long banquet table was in view. This was for her, the final frontier, her closing argument, the last conclusion—her ultimate last-minute attempt!

She would either fly like Supergirl or look like a buffoon trying. Mumbling the words "Up, up and away!" she surged off the table, arms straight in front of her, taking that familiar Supergirl pose. She did it! Margie was flying. Whether dreaming or not, this, for her, was Utopia. Glancing at the tables below and feeling the sensation of a bird, she was ecstatic—she was Supergirl! Her dream of being an Olympic runner was surpassed a million times over! She knew without a doubt that she had now touched the face of God!

Then, as she glanced back toward the front of the ballroom, she slammed headfirst into a hanging chandelier. Margie then evaporated into hundreds of crystal vapor particles and was sucked into one of the many crystals hanging on the chandelier. She reappeared as a tiny person in a Jim Beam bottle, sitting on a long dark purple couch with ruffles on the floor around the oval-shaped interior of the bottle. Pillows, blankets, and cushions brought a warm feeling, easing any anxiety Margie felt on the other side of that time warp. Sitting beside her was a beautiful woman wearing a skimpy pink-and-red harem outfit. The woman was in tears as Margie introduced herself.

"Hi, my name is Margie. What's your name?"

"I don't have a name; I'm just called Genie."

"Why are you crying, Genie?"

"I was abruptly ripped from my master Tony Nelson's house by my father and banished to this island called Patmos. Outside of my bottle is an old man named John who is now my master, but I am heartbroken over Tony."

Margie said to Genie, "I don't know where I am or where I am going. Can you help me get back to the ballroom where I came from, Genie?"

"Yes, but only with my master's approval can I help you."

Margie was now optimistic about her situation and asked Genie if they could talk with her new master.

"Sure," was Genie's reply as she folded her arms, squeezed her eyes shut, and nodded her head.

Poof! There they were standing in front of John as he was writing on a scroll. Genie spoke up and asked John if she could help Margie get back to her ballroom.

"Sure," he answered, "but only after you ladies let me know what your thoughts are on my latest revelations."

Both agreed to help John. John then asked them to listen as he read his recently finished writings.

"It is all over the place, so I will give you the synopsis," John told the ladies before beginning to read:

I, John, your brother and companion in the suffering and kingdom and patient endurance that are ours in Jesus, was on the island of Patmos because of the word of God and the testimony of Jesus. On the Lord's Day I was in the Spirit, and I heard behind me a loud voice like a trumpet, which said: "Write on a scroll what you see and send it to the seven churches: to Ephesus, Smyrna, Pergamum, Thyatira, Sardis, Philadelphia and Laodicea."

"Then, blah, blah, blah—I write a bunch of stuff about how bad they are."

Margie asked, "Could I leave now?"

"Wait," John answered. "I have just one more I want you to hear. How is this?"

Look, I am coming soon! My reward is with me, and I will give to each person according to what they have done. I am the Alpha and the Omega, the First and the Last, the Beginning and the End.

Blessed are those who wash their robes, that they may have the right to the tree of life and may go through the gates into the city.

Outside are the dogs, those who practice magic arts, the sexually immoral, the murderers, the idolaters and everyone who loves and practices falsehood. I, Jesus, have sent my angel to give you this testimony for the churches. I am the Root and the Offspring of David, and the bright Morning Star. The grace of the Lord Jesus be with God's people.

"Good stuff there, Johnny-boy, good stuff!" Margie continued, "Can I leave now?"

John looked at her with a confused expression and said, "Obviously, you do not understand the significance of this letter! Genie, send her back at once!"

With that, Genie folded her arms and squeezed her eyes shut.

"Wait!" Margie shouted. She looked at Genie and said, "I have a gift for you."

"A gift for me?" Genie looked surprised.

"Yes, it's a name."

Genie excitedly asked, "What's my name? What's my name?"

Margie looked at her and said, "Your name is Barbie."

"I love it! Thank you, Margie. Thank you!"

"You're welcome, Barbie."

Then, Barbie folded her arms, squeezed her eyes shut, and nodded her head—*poof*!

3

LITTLE PARABLE

Margie's return to the ballroom wasn't as uneventful as she hoped. She slammed once again into the chandelier, then tumbled down onto the golden floor. The chandelier then came crashing down onto the floor, shattering crystal glass throughout the picturesque ballroom.

As Margie staggered to her feet wobbly and dazed, she simultaneously shook glass off her body. She listened and looked around, only to realize that the Wild Dogs were no longer in the banquet hall.

She then saw the guest who swallowed up the basketball and asked, "Have you seen the boys I was chatting with earlier?"

"Yes, King Friday kicked them out of here."

"What?"

He went on to say:

When the king came in to see the guests, he noticed they were not wearing wedding clothes. He asked, "How did you guys get in here without wedding clothes?" They were speechless. Then the king told the attendants, "Tie them hand and foot, and throw them outside, into the darkness, where there will be weeping and gnashing of teeth." For many are invited, but few are chosen.

From the corner of her eye, she could see the attendees heading in her direction with a fierce look on their faces. Like her friends, she too was about to be thrown out into the darkness, but not before another change in a dimension.

Margie shut her eyes tightly as her lips begged to wake up from this unimaginable nightmare. But her wish was not to be. The scenery around her changed into a cold mountain desert area. Wobbling on her feet, with widened eyeballs, she encountered a giant warrior. He was wearing a bronze helmet with bronze on his legs. He was holding a bronze javelin that was strapped to his back. He had a sword that was as sharp as a razor. The giant's name was Goliath. He was screaming and belittling a young boy whose name was David. David was staring at Goliath as he put his hand into his bag that was strapped around his waist. Then he took out a pair of click-clacks and flung them, and hitting the great warrior in his forehead, the click-clacks sunk into his forehead; Goliath fell flat on his face.

Without hesitation, David ran over to Goliath and stood over him; he took the giant's sword from his belt and plunged it into his heart. Then, David cut off his head and held it high in the air. He turned in Margie's direction, and with a big smile on his face, he winked at her.

Her reaction was heart-throbbing terror. She took off running in the opposite direction and seeing a barn not far off in the distance, ran to it. Once inside, she climbed the ladder leading up to the hayloft, and she buried herself under piles of hay, hoping David wasn't following her.

Fifteen minutes later, she poked her head out from the hay, hoping all was clear. She noticed another hay pile only a few feet away shifting back and forth. The moving indicated to Margie that she was not alone. Not sure about the shifting hay pile, she took refuge back under her pile, where she would be safe for the moment.

As another fifteen minutes passed, not only was the other hay pile still shifting, but now she could hear soft sobbing from underneath it. Margie's curiosity won as she moved quietly toward the shifting pile. No longer able to contain herself, she began shoveling down into the hay. After a few good scoops, she grabbed hold of a short frisbee looking character. She picked up the character onto its knees as it wept uncontrollably.

"Hi," she said, "my name is Margie. What's your name?"

The frisbee character had a hard time speaking because of the continual crying.

"Calm down, everything is okay—I'm here now," Margie said. With that, it began to settle down and Margie asked again, "What's your name?"

Under a mountain of sniffles, it was able to muddle, "Parable, my name is Parable."

"Now that's a name I had never heard of before," Margie said.

"Yes, my teacher uses me all the time to get his point across."

"What do you mean Parable?" Margie asked.

"My teacher is incredibly wise, but this time I think he is asking for my life."

"Your life?"

"Yes, he just told a parable to a rich person—but I'm sure it was aimed at me also."

"Tell me the parable, Parable, and I will give you my opinion."

"Okay," Parable said. Then, in a soft Latin voice, she began to speak:

The ground of a certain rich man yielded an abundant harvest. He thought to himself, "What shall I do? I have no place to store my crops." Then he said, "This is what I'll do. I will tear down my barns and build bigger ones, and there I will store my surplus grain.

And I'll say to myself, 'You have plenty of grain laid up for many years.

Take life easy; eat, drink and be merry.'" But God said to him, "You fool! This very night your life will be demanded from you. Then who will get what you have prepared for yourself?" This is how it will be with whoever stores up things for themselves but is not rich toward God."

Margie started laughing as Parable was staring at her with the most serious look.

Margie explained, saying, "Parable, you are the parable—it is for the rich man to ponder, not you. Relax, you're not going to die."

Parable went on to tell Margie of other wiser parables, telling her, "And when they speak, I can't understand anything they say."

She wanted to know the meanings behind what some of the older and wiser parables meant. Margie settled into a comfortable position on a patch of hay and asked Parable for another parable.

Obliging, Parable said, "Here's one—they call it the Lamp." Parable continued:

You are the light of the world. A town built on a hill cannot be hidden. Neither do people light a lamp and put it under a bowl.

Instead they put it on its stand, and it gives light to everyone in the house. In the same way, let your light shine before others, that they may see your good deeds and glorify your Father in Heaven.

Just then, Margie and Parable noticed a third haystack shifting back and forth. Margie was in fear, thinking it was David, and Parable in fear, thinking it was the teacher. In sequence, on the count of three, they pounced onto the hay pile. Ruffling through the straw, they heard a loud, high-pitched squealing. Margie then grabbed hold of a human looking mouse by its throat. Choking and gurgling, the mouse tried to speak, but Margie's grip prevented that.

"Who are you! And what do you want!" Margie shouted.

As she released her grip, he began to speak.

"I'm Mickey from Orlando," squeaked back the six-fingered mouse wearing orange shorts, yellow shoes, and white gloves. The vermin went on to say he was also fearing for his life because of a certain thing he had heard in his household.

"Okay, okay, Mickey," Margie said. "What was it you heard that sent you into a hysteria, sending you to hide under the haystack like Parable and me?"

Mickey then repeated the words he had heard: *"They that sanctify themselves and purify themselves in the gardens behind one tree in the midst, eating swine's flesh, and the abomination, and the mouse shall be consumed together, saith the Lord."*

This time, both Margie and Parable broke out into side-aching laughter as Mickey shouted, "Why are you acting so goofy?"

"Oh, oh, we are sorry, Mickey, but that's funnier than what Parable had believed about her situation."

Mickey asked them to explain.

"Okay, after we finish listening to another parable from Parable," Margie said.

So, Margie and Mickey sat and listened.

Looking at Margie, Parable said, "Then there's this one called the Speck and the Log":

Do not judge, or you too will be judged. For in the same way you judge others, you will be judged, and with the measure you use, it will be measured to you. Why do you look at the speck of sawdust in your brother's eye and pay no attention to the plank in your own eye? How can you say to your brother, "Let me take the speck out of your eye," when all the time there is a plank in your own eye?

You hypocrite, first take the plank out of your own eye, and then you will see clearly to remove the speck from your brother's eye.

Parable then asked Margie: "Should I keep going?"

"Yes, please continue. I'm enjoying your wisdom."

"Okay, check this one out. It's called the Divided Kingdom":

*But when the Pharisees heard this, they said, "It is only by
  Beelzebub, the prince of demons, that this fellow drives out
  demons." The teacher knew their thoughts and said to them,
  "Every kingdom divided against itself will be ruined, and every city or
household divided against itself will not stand. If Satan drives out Satan, he
is divided against himself. How then can his kingdom stand?"*

Margie and Parable spoke continually, discussing one parable after another, until Margie's eyelids became heavy and she fell back onto the haystack fast asleep. Mickey quickly changed subjects and began telling Parable about a Magic Kingdom where dreams come true. Excitedly, Parable begged Mickey that they go there. With big smiles on their faces, Mickey picked up Parable and flung the frisbee out of the barn window. Then, Mickey jumped from the second story window, and both scooted off to find this Magic Kingdom.

Margie slept for hours, but when the time had come, she opened her eyes and watched as the loft beneath her was collapsing. Margie's landing found her in a courtroom setting with a screaming judge whose name was Judy. There was a delirious crowd of screaming spectators that filled the courtroom. Margie's eyes dotted back and forth, hoping for a sign of her friends.

With no luck, her ears burned in pain as the judge slammed her gavel, yelling, "Order in the court! Order in the court!"

The crowd immediately became silent as Judge Judy began to speak.

"In the case of *People v. Stevie the Blindman*, Plaintiff, please present your case."

The lawyer's name bringing the case was Perry Mason. He had established himself as a great lawyer in such cases as *Humpty Dumpty v. the Easter Egg* and *Red Riding Hood v. the Wolf*.

Mr. Mason began his opening statement with "Ladies and

gentlemen of the jury, this man Jesus saw a man named Stevie who was blind from birth." He continued:

And his disciples asked him, "Rabbi, who sinned, this man or his parents, that he was born blind?" Jesus answered, "It was not that this man sinned, or his parents, but that the works of God might be displayed in him. We must work the works of him who sent me while it is day; night is coming, when no one can work. As long as I am in the world, I am the light of the world." Having said these things, he spit on the ground and made mud with the saliva. Then he anointed Stevie's *eyes with the mud and said to him, "Go, wash in the pool of Siloam." So, he went and washed and came back seeing. Then,* Your Honor, the neighbors and *those who had seen him before as a beggar were saying, "Is this not* Stevie *who used to sit and beg?" Some said, "It is he." Others said, "No, but he is like him."* Stevie *kept saying, "I am the man." So, they said to him, "We wonder how your eyes were opened?" He answered, "The man called Jesus made mud and anointed my eyes and said to me,*

'Go to Siloam and wash.' So, I went and washed and received my sight." *They said to him, "Where is he?" He said, "I do not know."*

Mr. Mason continued to speak, saying, "Your Honor, I would like to call the blind man to the stand."

Looking toward the back of the courtroom, the judge spoke, saying, "Bring the blind man."

Margie looked around the room as she was confused not to see a blind man, but taking the stand was a man of good eyesight.

Mr. Mason had him raise his right hand and swore him in; then, he asked how he had received his sight.

He answered, *"He put mud on my eyes, and I washed, and I see."*

Mr. Mason said, *"This man is not from God, for he does not keep the Sabbath. How can a man who is a sinner do such signs?"* So, he said again to Stevie, *"What do you say about him, since he has opened your eyes?"*

Stevie said, *"He is a prophet."*

Mr. Mason did not believe that he had been blind and had received his sight. He then asked the judge for permission to call his parents.

"It is granted," said Judge Judy, as his parents Cliff and Claire stepped forward.

Promising to tell the truth, the whole truth, and nothing but the truth, they sat side by side on the bench.

Then, Mr. Mason asked them, "Is this your son, who you say was born blind? How then does he now see?"

His parents answered, *"We know that this is our son and that he was born blind. But how he now sees we do not know, nor do we know who opened his eyes. Ask him; he is of age. He will speak for himself."*

Frustrated with that answer, Mr. Mason called Stevie to the stand for the second time and said to him, *"Give glory to God. We know that this man is a sinner."*

Stevie answered, *"Whether he is a sinner, I do not know. One thing I do know, that though I was blind, now I see."*

Mr. Mason then said to him, *"What did he do to you? How did he open your eyes?"*

Stevie answered him, *"I have told you already, and you would not listen. Why do you want to hear it again? Do you also want to become his disciple?"*

Mr. Mason was now boiling in frustration and said, *"You are his disciple, but we are disciples of Moses. We know that God has spoken to Moses, but as for this man, we do not know where he comes from."*

Stevie answered, *"Why, this is an amazing thing! You do not know where he comes from, and yet he opened my eyes. We know that God does not listen to sinners, but if anyone is a worshiper of God and does his will, God listens to him. Never since the world began has it been heard that anyone opened the eyes of a man born blind. If this man were not from God, he could do nothing."*

Mr. Mason was now out of control, tossing tables and chairs, saying, *"You were born in utter sin, and would you teach us?"*

He grabbed Stevie by the seat of his pants and threw him out of the courtroom! Margie ran to Stevie's side, asking many questions about his experience. He repeated those words he spoke inside the courtroom. Margie then walked with Stevie to the house of his friend Bartimaeus.

Before reaching the house, Stevie saw Jesus and ran to him.

"I heard how you were cast out of the courtroom," Jesus said. *"Do you believe in the Son of Man?"*

He answered, "And who is he, sir, that I may believe in him?"

Jesus said to him, "You have seen him, and it is he who is speaking to you."

He said, "Lord, I believe," and he worshiped him.

Jesus said, "For judgment, I came into this world, that those who do not see may see, and those who see may become blind."

4

GILLIGAN

Jesus looked at Margie, and immediately her eyes began to sting and tear up—she became blind. With a blast of "Hey Margie!" her eyesight returned, and she then stumbled and fell into a huge caterpillar cocoon. She was trapped on the inside of it, with caterpillars covering her from head to toe.

Margie was now going with each adventure, accepting the good and bad, and remembering what the Wild Dogs had told her: "Margie, you are dead!"

Margie was in the season of transformation between a caterpillar and a butterfly. She felt herself being lifted several feet off the ground inside of the cocoon as the once caterpillars changed into butterflies and began flapping their tiny wings. Then the cocoon burst like a bubble, sending hundreds of butterflies into the air as Margie dropped to the ground.

Trying to ignore her aches and pains, she lay flat on her back, looking toward the sky and watching as thousands of butterflies ascended into the heavens. Loud yelling interrupted her fascination with the butterflies as she heard two men arguing.

"I will not let you go unless you bless me," one of the men shouted.

In response, the second man said, *"What is your name?"*

"Jacob," he answered.

The second man then said, *"Your name will no longer be Jacob, but Israel, because you have struggled with God and with humans and have overcome."*

Jacob said, "Please tell me your name."

But the man replied, "Why do you ask my name?"

Then the second man blessed him there. So, *Jacob called the place Peniel, saying, "It is because I saw God face to face, and yet my life was spared."*

Jacob walked away limping as Margie was shaking her head in disbelief. She watched the second man turn into a mammoth butterfly and fly off in the same direction as the others. Margie's sensors and emotions spun in circles as she tried desperately to grasp her thoughts. At the same time, she was feeling dizzy and sat down, hoping for some rest.

Margie delved into the distance and saw the butterfly returning toward her. Having no energy to get up, she stayed on the ground and watched the butterfly land on a nearby mountainside.

She then heard oxygen being sucked into a long plastic Krazy Straw just below the eyes of the butterfly. From the end of the straw, words began to drip out of it and onto the ground.

These were the words:

Blessed are those who are persecuted for righteousness' sake, for theirs is the kingdom of heaven. Blessed are the peacemakers, for they shall be called sons of God. Blessed are those who mourn, for they shall be comforted. Blessed are the pure in heart, for they shall see God. Blessed are the meek, for they shall inherit the earth. Blessed are the merciful, for they shall receive mercy.

Blessed are the poor in spirit, for theirs is the kingdom of heaven.

Blessed are those who hunger and thirst for righteousness, for they shall be satisfied.

. . .

As more words were about to drip from the butterfly's straw, a monstrous python appeared from behind it and swallowed it in one mouthful. The butterfly, although consumed, was still alive within the snake's belly. Margie could hear a conversation going on between the serpent and butterfly within the belly.

The serpent shouted, "If you are Him, *tell these stones to become bread.*"

Mr. Butterfly answered, *"It is written they shall not live on bread alone, but on every word that comes from my mouth."*

The snake snapped right back after dragging the butterfly to the highest point in the city and said, *"If you are the Son of God, throw yourself down. For it is written: 'He will command his angels concerning you, and they will lift you up in their hands so that you will not strike your foot against a stone.'"*

The butterfly replied, *"It is also written: 'Do not put the Lord your God to the test.'"*

Again, the snake took him to another very high point and showed him all the kingdoms of the world and their splendor.

"All this I will give you," he said, *"if you will bow down and worship me."*

Mr. Butterfly said to him, "Away from me, bad snake! *For it is written: 'Worship the Lord your God and serve him only.'"*

Then the python regurgitated Mr. Butterfly and watched as two angels came and attended to him while two other angels grabbed Margie by her arms and swished her away into the darkness.

They *arrived at a city called Sodom in the evening,* and a man named *Lot was sitting in the gateway of the city.* When he saw Margie and the angels, *he got up to meet them and bowed down with his face to the ground,* making Margie feel as if now she were royalty.

"My lords," he said, *"please turn aside to your servant's house. You can wash your feet and spend the night and then go on your way early in the morning."*

"No," they answered, *"we will spend the night in the square."*

As Margie looked around, she no longer felt like royalty, realizing that she was now in the worst part of town. *He insisted so strongly that they did go with him and enter his house. He prepared a meal for them, baking bread without yeast, and they ate.*

Before they had gone to bed, all the men from every part of the city of Sodom—both young and old—surrounded the house. They called to Lot, "Where are the men who came to you tonight?"

Margie listened with her ear to the door and heard what Lot was saying, then broke out into a cold sweat, yelling at Lot: "Are you insane?" *I'm not going out there! Those men are crazy!*

Then she heard the men say to Lot: *"Get out of our way. This fellow came here as a foreigner, and now he wants to play the judge! We'll treat you worse than them."*

They kept bringing pressure on Lot and moved forward to break down the door. But the men inside reached out and pulled Lot back into the house and shut the door. Then they struck the men who were at the door of the house, young and old, with blindness so that they could not find the door.

Early the next morning they looked down toward Sodom and Gomorrah, toward all the land of the plain, and he saw dense smoke rising from the land, like smoke from a furnace.

Margie stood there, hoping to remove herself from Lot and his family. Although she was told not to look back, Margie did so and watched as Lot and his family turned into glitter, falling harmlessly onto the ground. That harmless glitter, Margie soon found out, wasn't so harmless. The glitter turned into two tiny Power Rangers, one named Trini and the other Kimberly. Each spun with a mighty force, digging themselves down into Margie's eardrums. Trini dug deep into the right ear and Kimberly into the left, both wrapping themselves around Margie's vocal cords, causing her to strangle and pass out.

Waking up with one bad sore throat, she found herself locked in a cabin on a ship called the S. S. *Minnow.* She could hear squabbling and the names Gilligan and Skipper tossed back and forth like a hot potato. Margie began yelling in a whisper, at the same time banging on the door trying to get the crew's attention.

It was obvious to her from their arguing that the ship and its crew were lost at sea. She stopped banging on the cabin door and put her ear to it.

She heard Skipper shout, "Gilligan, *weigh anchor! And sail along the shore.*"

Margie could hear her cabin being unlocked from the other side of the door and stepped aside and watched as a young woman grabbed a fleece from the bed.

As the woman turned around, she was startled by Margie, throwing the fleece right into her face, screaming, "You scared me half to death!"

Margie, who was now giggling, apologized and introduced herself: "Hi, I'm Margie from the Golden Graveyard."

The woman identified herself as Mary Ann and went on to say there were six others aboard. Mary Ann took Margie to the upper deck and introduced her to Gilligan, the Skipper, Mr. and Mrs. Howell, Ginger, and the Professor. All were preoccupied trying to stay alive.

Before very long, a wind of hurricane force, called the Northeaster, swept down from a nearby island. The ship was caught by the storm and could not head into the wind; so, they gave way to it and were driven along. As they passed the small island, they were hardly able to make the lifeboat secure, so the crew hoisted it aboard. Then they passed ropes under the ship itself to hold it together. Because they were afraid they would run aground on the sandbars, they lowered the sea anchor and let the ship be driven along. Margie had now become seasick, puking with the shakes and shivers in a lower cabin.

On the third day, they threw the ship's tackle overboard with their own hands. When neither sun nor stars appeared for many days and the storm continued raging, they finally gave up all hope of being saved.

After they had gone a long time without food, Gilligan *stood up before them and said,* "Folks, you should have taken my advice not to sail out of Lulu; *then you would have spared yourselves this damage and loss. But now I urge you to keep up your courage, because not one of us will be lost; only the ship will be destroyed.*"

Feeling better now, Margie re-emerged to the upper deck, listening to Gilligan give an encouraging talk.

"*Last night an angel of the God to whom I belong and whom I serve stood beside me and said, 'Do not be afraid, Gilligan. God has graciously given you the lives of all who sail with you.' So, keep up your courage, folks, for I have faith in God that it will happen just as he told me. Nevertheless, we must run aground on some island.*"

Then, Gilligan said to the Howells: "*Unless you stay with the ship, you cannot be saved.*" So, Gilligan *cut the ropes that held the lifeboat and let it drift away.*

Cutting loose the anchors, he left them in the sea and at the same time untied the ropes that held the rudders. Then he hoisted the foresail to the wind and made for the beach. But the ship struck a sandbar and ran aground.

Skipper *ordered those who could swim to jump overboard first and get to land. The rest were to get there on planks or on other pieces of the ship. In this way, everyone reached land safely.* Margie, being an excellent swimmer, did the backstroke all the way to land. *Once* all were *safely on shore, they found out that the island was called Malta. The islanders showed them unusual kindness.*

The islanders built a fire and welcomed them all because it was raining and cold. Margie *gathered a pile of brushwood and, as she put it on the fire, a viper, driven out by the heat, fastened itself on her hand. When the islanders saw the snake hanging from her hand, they said to each other, "This girl must be a murderer; for though she escaped from the sea, our goddess Justice has not allowed her to live."*

But Margie *shook the snake off into the fire and suffered no ill effects. The islanders expected her to swell up or suddenly fall dead; but after waiting a long time and seeing nothing unusual happen to her, they changed their minds and said she was a goddess. There was an estate nearby that belonged to the chief official of the island. He welcomed them to his home and showed them generous hospitality for three days.*

His father was sick in bed, suffering from fever and dysentery. Gilligan *went in to see him and, after prayer, placed his hands on him and healed him. When this had happened, the rest of the sick on the island came and were cured. They honored the crew in many ways; and when they were ready to sail, they furnished them with the supplies needed.*

Boarding the ship to leave, out from the forest came a small black terrier barking up a storm. The dog jumped right into Margie's arms, licking her face nonstop. Margie reminisced about that morning when her Dobermans acted in similar fashion. The word *Toto* could be heard coming from the forest. Margie instructed the Skipper to wait while she returned the lost dog.

As Margie ran into the woods holding the little terrier, a woman whose name was Dorothy approached her, obviously distressed and confused, shouting, "Toto!"

Margie handed Dorothy Toto, and Dorothy took off running deeper into the thicket, shouting to a hot air balloon drifting in the sky: "Wait for me! Wait for me!"

Margie made her way back onto the beach, only to discover the ship had sailed without her. Loneliness and sadness now consumed Margie as she turned and slowly walked back into the forest. How she now missed those ferocious Dobermans pounding her to the ground. She was now both scared and paranoid, aimlessly walking past several waterfalls, lakes, and flowering trees. Margie came upon a familiar site; it was a baseball field. Her mind raced back to the days Dad would take her to the ball game, and those words rang out in her head:

Take me out to the ball game,
Take me out with the crowd.
Buy me some peanuts and Cracker Jack,
I don't care if I never get back,
Let me root, root, root for the home team,
If they don't win, it's a shame.
For it's one, two, three strikes, you're out,
At the old ball game.

The sign above the field read, "Angels Minor League Club." Twelve players and their manager flippantly tossed baseballs to one another in a casual manner.

As Margie walked onto the field, the players and manager took notice of her immediately.

The players continued their activities as the manager walked over and asked, "Are you the scout?" He continued, "My name is Yogi Berra. What's yours?"

"Margie," she answered. "I'm looking for clarification."

As she was about to continue, Yogi interrupted her and said, "You're from the Majors! I have some excellent talent here that I want you to see!"

Before Margie could speak, Yogi had the players lined up, and one by one, they gave a short glimpse of their talents.

"Hi, I'm *Hosea*: the world's greatest love story."

"Hi, I'm *Joel*: a wake-up call."

"Hi, I'm *Amos*: how God sees us today."

"Hi, I'm *Obadiah*: how God deals with pride."

"Hi, I'm *Jonah*: struggling with God and God's concern for all people."

"Hi, I'm *Micah*: what God expects of us."

"Hi, I'm *Nahum*: what hurts the heart of God."

"Hi, I'm *Habakkuk*: Dear God, I have a question."

"Hi, I'm *Zephaniah*: how God works in our lives."

"Hi, I'm *Haggai*: perseverance to finish the job when enthusiasm is fading."

"Hi, I'm *Zechariah*: being God's people."

"Hi, I'm *Malachi*: giving God our best."

"No! I'm not a scout, and I'm not from the Majors!" Margie shouted. "I'm from the Golden Graveyard, and all I want is clarification on where I am!"

With a giggle, he said, "Oh! Why didn't you just say so in the first place, Margie?"

Disgruntled and fighting fatigue, she stormed off the field. Exhausted and no longer able to walk, she plunged herself upon a patch of the softest, most comfortable green grass she had ever felt.

She lay there listening to the sounds of birds whistling and crickets chirping. Margie listened closely as the trees around her began to whisper tiny soft-spoken words that placed her into a deep trance.

These were the words that gently massaged her ears while she dozed off into Never Never Land:

Remain in me, as I also remain in you. No branch can bear fruit by itself; it must remain in the vine. Neither can you bear fruit unless you remain in me. I am the vine; you are the branches. If you remain in me and I in you, you will bear much fruit; apart from me you can do nothing. If you do not remain in me, you are like a branch that is thrown away and withers; such branches are picked up, thrown into the fire and burned. If you remain in me and my words remain in you, ask whatever you wish, and it will be done for you. This is to my Father's glory, that you bear much fruit, showing yourself to be my daughter.

When Margie awoke, she found herself amid a garden, which was sprouting graham crackers. With her breakfast delight everywhere around her, she began munching them down as fast as possible— until she tried to pluck the next cracker, and it refused to release itself from its vine.

The cracker then began speaking, "What do you think you're doing? Have you not a heart? Why are you devouring our village?"

Margie just stood there with the graham cracker crumbs flaking off her lips, and said, "Oh, I'm so sorry. I was starving and didn't realize what I was doing."

The graham cracker cracked back at her: "We forgive you, little lady. Who are you? And what do you want from us?"

"My name is Margie, and I'm looking for my friends. Have you seen them?"

"Yes, they were here at last night's crusade, but they took off just after my tenth notable quote."

Margie asked the graham his name and what the ten notable quotes were. He introduced himself as Billy, the Graham Cracker Crusader. He told her that his quotes helped nourish and sustain his fellow crackers. He asked if she would like to hear them.

"Definitely!" she replied, adding that she needed much sustaining and nourishment. Then, in a booming voice, Billy Graham Cracker began to preach, giving her lines from some of his most famous sermons.

"When wealth is lost, nothing is lost; when health is lost, something is lost; when character is lost, all is lost."

"My home is in Heaven. I'm just traveling through this world."

"Courage is contagious. When a brave man takes a stand, the spines of others are often stiffened."

"God has given us two hands, one to receive and the other to give with."

"Nothing can bring a real sense of security into the home except true love."

"Tears shed for self are tears of weakness, but tears shed for others are a sign of strength."

"A child who is allowed to be disrespectful to his parents will not have true respect for anyone."

"When granted many years of life, growing old in age is natural, but growing old with grace is a choice."

"Racial prejudice, anti-Semitism, or hatred of anyone with different beliefs has no place in the human mind or heart."

"The word 'romance,' according to the dictionary, means excitement, adventure, and something extremely real. Romance should last a lifetime."

After Billy finished, Margie's attention was diverted when she felt a soft touch to her cheek. Then, her face was poked and licked by a long tongue, and after a few more good licks to her face, she was wiped from the Graham Garden and into the presence of a fifteen-foot speaking giraffe, who identified himself as Geoffrey.

In turn, Margie identified herself once again as "Margie from the Golden Graveyard." Geoffrey then asked her to follow him to his secret place. His secret place was a toy-land of apple trees. Margie agreed and hopped on Geoffrey's back and rode him like a horse. Galloping a good distance, they reached the toy-land of apple trees. Geoffrey was the perfect height to reach the apples, so he began munching and crunching away to his heart's delight.

Margie then heard yelling and screaming from behind the trees. Not sure what to do next, she just stopped. It was a couple arguing like children on a playground.

Then, she heard a third, much louder voice say, *"Where are you?"*

The other answered, *"I heard you in the garden, and I was afraid because I was naked; so, I hid."*

The third voice spoke and said, *"Who told you that you were naked? Have you eaten from the tree that I commanded you not to eat from?"*

Then, Geoffrey started to cry because at once all the apples rotted away. The earth started shaking as lightning began to appear. Ocean-sized buckets of water began pouring down from the sky. Within minutes, the water was up to Geoffrey's neck, and rising quickly. Margie's mind was racing as for what to do, remembering when her teacher had told her that giraffes couldn't swim. Margie watched helpless as her friend Geoffrey drowned as the water surpassed his head.

Margie would have been the next drowning victim, but being a good swimmer, she once again started swimming on her back. Looking up at the bright blue sky, she noticed a dove flying high above her. She watched as the dove dropped an *Olive leaf*, which slowly drifted downward, landing right on her forehead. With her eyes crossed, looking up at the leaf, it took the shape of a frog. The frog then leaped from her forehead onto a lily pad. Margie realized that she also was floating on a lily pad. Being able to sit up on the water, she looked around and saw hundreds of lily pads surrounding her, each home to its own frog.

The frog next to her began singing a beautiful song:

> Why are there so many songs about rainbows
> And what's on the other side
> Rainbows are visions
> But only illusions
> And rainbows have nothing to hide

As the frog continued to sing, a beautiful rainbow appeared, stretching from one side of the ocean to the other. Then, chiming in from the heavens blending masterfully in harmony, a second voice sang:

> *I have set my rainbow in the clouds, and it will be the sign*
> *of the covenant between me and the earth.*
> *Whenever I bring clouds over the earth and the rainbow*
> *appears in the clouds, I will remember my covenant*
> *between me and you and all living creatures of every kind.*

> *Never again will the waters become a flood to destroy all life.*
> *Whenever the rainbow appears in the clouds,*
> *I will see it and remember the everlasting covenant between*
> *God and all living creatures of every kind on the earth.*

As the two voices ended the song, the frog said, "I think that was so beautiful."

The other voice said, "I think so too, Kermit."

The song lulled Margie into a daze as she fell back onto her lily pad. As Margie continued to float on her back, she could feel vibrations causing her to flip over to her stomach.

What next? Would Margie float like a boat? Or would she sink with a blink? No more flip-flopping—here she goes!

5

FIRE

Without warning, from the deep waters appeared Moby Dick the gigantic whale with his mouth wide open, and he began to devour Margie. As she was being sucked down into the whale's belly, she could hear a sailor encouraging her to grab hold of one of the whale's ribs. Margie quickly did as she was told and attached herself to a rib. She was swayed back and forth with her arms and legs wrapped around that rib for dear life.

Then—quiet. All was silent as Margie slid herself from the whale's rib to a solid part of its fish guts. As she walked around the fish guts, she could hear soft-spoken voices in the distance, and she caught a glimpse of a ray of light. Following the light, she came upon a middle-aged man talking to a red crab. To her astonishment, the crab was talking back to the man. Staring at both the man and crab, she was politely invited into the conversation.

The crab then spoke in a Jamaican accent: "Hi! My name is Bastian, and my friend here is Jonah!"

Margie introduced herself to the pair and sat down between them. She then asked Jonah: "Have we met before? You look awfully familiar."

Jonah answered that he didn't believe so.

Margie then asked, "Can you tell me where I am and what's going on? And is there a way out of here?"

Bastian quickly answered, "You can get out of here if Mr. Stubborn would do the right thing!"

Jonah sat quietly as Margie asked, "What does he need to do?"

Bastian spoke up and said, "He needs to repent!"

"What for?"

"Oh! He got himself in a pickle with God and is too proud to do the right thing!"

She dropped to her knees and pleaded with Jonah: "Please! Please do the right thing, Jonah!" She then began to weep.

With a quick response, Jonah said, "Okay! Okay! Just stop sniffling."

Jonah then got down on his knees and began to pray with these words:

I call out to you, Lord in my mess. From the belly of the underworld I cry out for help. You had cast me into the depths in the heart of the seas, and a flood surrounds me. All your strong waves and rushing water pass over me. So, I say, "I have been driven away from your sight. Will I ever again be looked upon with grace? Waters have engulfed me to the point of death; the deep surrounds me. Seaweed is wrapped around my head. I have sunk down to the underworld; its bars hold me with no end in sight.

But you can bring me out of this mess." When my endurance was weakening, I remembered you Lord, and my prayers come to you. Those deceived by worthless things lose their chance for mercy. But me, I will offer a sacrifice to you with a voice of thanks. That which I have promised, I will do. Deliverance belongs to you, my Lord!

As his prayer ended instantaneously, with one painful contraction, the whale caused Margie, Jonah, Bastian, and tons of seawater to come gushing out of the whale's blowhole, lifting them high into the air. Bouncing on top of bubbling water, Margie noticed Jonah and Bastian had vanished.

The bubbling water then turned into a lake where she found herself aboard a tiny boat in the darkness. Margie could hear men yelling out to a ghostly figure that was walking on the lake.

Terrified, they cried out in fear: "It's a ghost!"

She looked intently as goosebumps on top of goosebumps spread throughout her body.

The ghost-like man immediately said to them: *"Take courage! It is I. Don't be afraid."*

Then, one of the men answered back: *"Lord, if it's you, tell me to come to you on the water."*

"Come," the ghostly figure said.

The man got down out of the boat, walked on the water, and came toward the ghostly figure.

But when the man saw the wind, he was afraid and, beginning to sink, cried out, *"Lord, save me!"* Immediately, the ghost-man reached out his hand and caught him.

"You of little faith," he said, *"why did you doubt?" And when they climbed into the boat, the wind died down.*

Then, those who were in the boat began worshipping him, saying, *"Truly you are the Son of God."*

Not knowing what else to do, Margie fell to her knees, shouting out, "Truly you are the Son of God. Truly you are the Son of God."

At once, the ghost and the men stopped and turned to Margie, asking her: "Who are you, and where do you come from?"

She answered, "I am Margie, and I come from the Golden Graveyard."

With stone-cold faces, they picked her up, and as she began to yell and scream, they threw her overboard into the darkness of night.

As Margie was panicking and gasping for air, she felt a squishy squirminess below her feet. It was mud from the bottom of the lake. She then realized the water was only waist deep, so she stood up.

Looking toward the sky, she watched as it shined brighter and brighter. Appearing from the brightest star was a ladder hanging from the heavens, carrying people who sprouted wings, ascending and descending on the ladder.

The people shouted her name, saying, "Margie—Margie! Hop on!"

Indecisiveness clouded her brain, and by sheer instinct, she grabbed the lower rung of the ladder. She was lifted to what the winged people were calling the third heaven. Margie was baffled that she had missed the first and second heaven.

Astonished and not believing her eyes or ears, she heard shouts of "Heigh-ho, heigh-ho, it's down to hell we go!"

But there they were, singing on their way down—Jose, Skittles, Lucas, and Pits, hanging by a skyhook connected to their waist belts. Before she could call out to them, the skyhook snapped, sending the Wild Dogs into a free fall. In a flash before her eyes, she knew that the Wild Dogs, along with herself, could conquer this space-time continuum. Margie had now let go of that bottom rung of the ladder herself. So, both Margie and the Wild Dogs were helplessly twirling toward the earth. That landing was brutal—their bodies slammed one on top of the other, propping up like a pyramid of dirty flesh. Their landing spot was dark, smelly, and cold. After a few minutes, their eyes adjusted to the darkness, and then they realized all were now prisoners in a dungeon. Heavy metal bars caged them in like animals, and in the distance, they could hear singing.

The tunes were praises like melodies to God. They could see soldiers heading in their direction. One soldier was holding a bucket, and one was wielding a large half-moon looking sword. The rattling of large keys was followed by instructions to step back to the rear of their cell. One soldier grabbed Lucas by his neck and applied pressure, causing intense pain that paralyzed his body. The others cowered in the corner as Lucas was held down by three other soldiers. The bucket was then placed under Lucas' head. Trying to escape, the group rushed the soldiers in one motion. They were massively overpowered and hurled back into the corner of their cell.

Lucas was screaming and crying for his life as another soldier, holding the half-moon sword, took a couple of practice swings through the air. At that point, there was nothing Lucas or the others could do. They watched in horror as the sword-holding soldier let loose with one mighty swing, slicing Lucas' head right off his shoulders like a hot knife slicing through butter.

His head bounced several times up and down, splattering blood everywhere before finally coming to a halt inside the bucket. Pits passed out from the gruesome sight while the rest crumbled in fear at the back of the cell.

Next, the soldiers grabbed Skittles, pulling him from the cell as he shook, trembled, and convulsed with fear. Two soldiers held his head down into the bucket containing the head of Lucas. Skittles was now staring into the eyeballs of his dead buddy. Screams and mercy pleads were ignored, and the last thing Skittles would see was the decapitated head of his friend Lucas. With one whack, the soldiers succeeded with their version of a doubleheader. Only this time, Skittles' head bounced off the side of the bucket and rolled onto the dungeon floor straight toward them as they watched in horror.

The soldiers kicked the head of Skittles like it was a soccer ball, sending it crashing into the brick wall just behind them. The soldiers, grinning with wide evil smirks, turned and grabbed Jose. He was dragged to the front of the cell and like Skittles, he kicked, screamed, and begged for his life. Other soldiers came marching down the hall. One was carrying a bucket of kerosene that sent heavy odors of the substance throughout the dungeon.

Jose was now on his stomach face down, slamming his head against the cobblestone floor trying to knock himself out. Several soldiers snatched Jose from the floor and hoisted him onto a sharp metal hook sticking out of the wall. The kerosene bucket was dumped over his body, drenching him in kerosene. In the distance, Margie could see another soldier heading Jose's way, carrying a torch giving more light to see throughout the dungeon.

Margie looked around into the other cells and saw men, women, and children, half-dead from starvation, moving slowly about and gurgling white foam from their mouths. The torch was then waved under Jose's feet, igniting him into flames. Agonizing screams of terror blasted off the brick walls while the stench of burned flesh filled the air.

Appearing before Margie only a few feet away stood a five-foot three-hundred-pound lion, looking awfully hungry. Margie's fate was now to be eaten alive by that mighty lion. Margie ran to the passed-out Pits and desperately tried to revive him, crying for help. As the lion slowly stepped in her direction, his mouth grew larger and larger. She fell onto the floor, waiting for the inevitable to come.

Then, she heard the sweetest words imaginable: "Hey Margie! Hey Margie!"

And as quick as a flicker of light, there she was standing under an olive tree with human-sized olives bursting with ripeness. After what Margie had just experienced, she was now living in a New York state of mind. From this point on, she resolved that she would not let herself bend to fear! Thick as a brick and as soil to oil, there sat an olive, attached to a scroll. The scroll read, "Five worthy pits, open with care." That olive was as soft as a feather, with honey dripping from its side. Margie reached her arm deep into the olive and grabbed hold of the five pits. When she took out the pits, she placed them on the floor. They began to bicker with each other in squeaky, high-pitched voices. The group argued over whose pit was worthy of the scroll trophy.

Margie hushed the pits to silence, then asked, "What the heck is going on here?"

One pit stepped forward and said, "We are scroll pits, and we are trying to find out which one of us is worthy for the Scroll Bowl."

Margie said, "Is this some sort of contest?"

"Yes," the pit who stepped forward answered. The pit added, "Can you be the judge?"

Margie thought for a minute then figured, as ridiculous as it was, she determined herself to stick it out.

She asked, "What is it I am to judge?"

He answered, "Where you find the word *pits*, undeniably superior to the others in the scroll, then, and only then, will that pit be declared the winner of the Pit Trophy. Each of us will recite three scroll verses containing the word *pits*, so listen closely."

"Okay, let's do this," Margie said.

The first pit stated, "My first verse is *Genesis 14:10*: '*Now the Valley of Siddim contained many asphalt pits, and as the kings of Sodom and Gomorrah fled, some fell into them, but the rest fled to the mountains.*'"

"My second verse is *Genesis 37:20*: '*Come on, let's kill him and throw him into one of the pits.*'"

"My third is *1 Samuel 13:6*: '*When the men of Israel saw that they were in a strait, (for the people were distressed,) then the people did hide themselves in caves, and in thickets, and in rocks, and in high places, and in pits and cisterns.*'"

Then, the second pit stepped forward in a squeaky, sarcastic tone and said, "Stand back, Green Lantern, I've got the winner." Reciting his first verse, he began, "*2 Samuel 17:19*: '*Lo, now, he is hidden in one of the pits, or in one of the places, and it hath been, at the falling among them at the commencement, that the hearer hath heard, and said, 'There hath been a slaughter among the people who are after Absalom.*'"

Then, the number the two pit boasted, "My second verse is even better than the first! *2 Kings 23:24*: '*Josiah also got rid of the ritual pits used to conjure up spirits, the magicians, personal idols, disgusting images, and all the detestable idols that had appeared in the land of Judah and in Jerusalem.*'"

"And my third is *Psalm 107:20*: '*He sent them an assuring word and healed them; he rescued them from the pits where they were trapped.*'"

Then, the third pit stepped forward, but before he could start his sentence, he began to shake and convulse while growing larger and larger. Then, pit number three turned into a blistering, red jelly blobby gob. Then the blobby gob began to mold itself into a human being. Appearing before her eyes now stood the teen Pits—full of red blobby gob.

Margie shouted, "Pits!"

Her commanding voice liquified the entire area, turning everything into green pea soup. Swallowing gulps of the green soup,

Margie coughed and choked, and with the blink of an eye, she found herself standing on a road in a desolate area all alone. Terrorized and discombobulated with green puke dripping from her lips, Margie started to walk the road, hoping it would lead to somewhere safe.

Her mind was wandering as she thought about Pits, *when* she *was attacked by robbers. They stripped* her *of* her *clothes, beat* her, *and went away, leaving* her *half dead. A priest happened to be going down the same road, and when he saw* Margie, he passed by on the other side. *So too,* another man, *when he came to the place and saw* her, passed by on the other side. But a good guy named Mr. Gump, *as he traveled, came where* she *was; and when he saw* her, he took pity on *her. He went to* her *and bandaged* her *wounds, pouring on oil and wine. Then, he put* Margie *on his own donkey, brought* her *to an inn, and took care of her. The next day, he took out* five gold coins *and gave* it *to the innkeeper.*

"Look after her," *he said, "and when I return, I will reimburse you for any extra expense you may have."*

She was treated like a queen at the inn—the hospitality she received was magnificent, and the good folks there even covered and adorned her with a beautiful coat of many colors.

6

ACNE

Margie believed it was too good to be true. She was right! Biff and Peggy's beautiful daughter was grabbed from behind, stripped of that beautiful coat, and thrown down into a dark, damp well. She survived the fall but was shivering and bewildered.

Looking up to the opening of the well, she could see several men looking back down at her, snickering and dribbling insults toward her, saying, *"We shall say, 'Some wild beast has devoured her.' We shall see what will become of her dreams!"*

For some absurd reason, they took pity on her and tossed a rope down, allowing Margie to climb back up to freedom. The rope had knots on it every few feet, allowing for a good grip and easy climb out. When she reached the top, several of the men grabbed her, then slapped and shoved her into the side of a donkey. She was then tied to that donkey.

Margie was now part of a small traveling caravan of men, women, and children, along with a few camels and sheep. Her head was squashed facing downward toward the road, so she could only see dirt and mud. She was like a trapped animal, taken away to be mocked and shamed without pity. The man walking beside her directed the donkey away from the caravan, bringing Margie onto a narrow path where they stopped. She heard the man screaming at his donkey.

In turn, the donkey opened his mouth and said, *"What have I done to you to make you beat me these three times?"*

The man shouted back, *"You have made a fool of me! If only I had a sword in my hand, I would kill you right now."*

The conversation ended as the man became timid a few minutes later. The pain of rope burns from the shifting ropes scorched her body as they returned to the caravan. Palms were appearing below the feet of the donkey, and shouts of joy blasted from both sides of the road.

She was able to see shadows of people and hear people shouting, *"Hosanna to the Son of David! Blessed is he who comes in the name of the Lord! Hosanna in the highest heaven!"*

Those wonderful words comforted her body and healed the rope burns. The ropes dissolved, and she was now able to sit straight up. Margie evaluated her condition and found it favorable, considering her previous situation. She was just wishing for a few minutes of peace. That peace never came as a bright light from the sky began to flash all around her. She was knocked from the donkey's back and onto the floor.

Suddenly, a light shone around her *from heaven. Then* she *fell to the ground, and* she *heard a voice saying to* her, *"Margie, Margie, why are you persecuting Me?"*

And she *said, "Who are You, Lord?"*

Then the Lord said, "I am Jesus, whom you are persecuting. It is hard for you to kick against the goads."

So Margie, *trembling and astonished, said, "Lord, what do You want me to do?"*

She was told to go down a straight street, to a certain old woman's house, where she would find chestnuts roasting on an open fire. At this point, she was getting frightfully excited about all the things going on around her. It didn't take long before Margie reached the straight street and found the house described.

She looked through the window and saw chestnuts roasting on an open fire. Then, a tiny cloud appeared before her nose with frost gently nipping at it. Posted on the door, a sign read "Yuletide Carols." Not sure about going into the house, she stood outside, poking her head into the window.

She watched as a woman fiddling with the fireplace stood listening to a voice from the flames say, *"I AM WHO I AM."*

The old woman in the house tried in vain to douse the flames with a nearby bucket of water. The task was not only unsuccessful, but the flames reached out to grab her. Margie watched in horror as the flames engulfed the old woman's apron as she was racing out the doorway. Margie then was sucked into the window as a heavy wind pushed her toward the fireplace. Tripping over a pile of wood logs in the middle of the floor, she tumbled into the raging fire. The logs immediately stuck to Margie's body, and she was burning alive. As skin melted from her body, she could hear her voice screaming for help—not only was she being burned alive, but she could not pass out.

Margie was now totally aware of the intense pain lashing her body. The flames continued to toast her like a marshmallow, and any tears she had were evaporated immediately. She heard cries of howling laughter from below her. This went on for hours and days, as she was burned alive continually. The pain and suffering would not let up, as her body was in a constant rejuvenated state of burning to death, but never ending.

Margie realized that she could neither pass out nor die in this agonizing state. She did think about Jose, bursting into flames back in the dungeon and wondered if he, like her, was still burning to death. It took a while, but she figured from the words above the flame "Easy Bake Oven" that her torture chamber was a fiery furnace, cranked up to an unfathomable temperature.

Her eyelids could have popped off her melting face when she saw five men dancing to the Irish jig with glee within the middle of the furnace. Her agony and painful situation changed in a flash as she was still consumed with flames throughout her body, but the pain had dissipated as she looked upon the five overjoyed, zealous human figures dancing to the jig.

She recognized one of the five to be Jose. Last time she saw Jose, he was engulfed in flames. Now she was watching him jump for joy within a blasting furnace dancing to the Irish jig. Jose grabbed onto Margie's hands, instantly infusing into her mind a full understanding of the Irish jig. They danced in a circle while holding hands, bouncing, and singing delightful tunes celebrating their camaraderie. Trumpets then blasted around them that caused the wall of flames to collapse, changing the scenery from flames to a brick wall.

Margie and Jose found themselves marching within a military regiment, shouting from the top of their lungs as the blast of trumpets continued. They walked for what seemed like an eternity. Margie was struck with a queasy feeling of déjà vu about the wall. Then, one final blast from the trumpet, and one last loud scream from the roaring crowd. Without a warning or indication, the wall crumbled to the ground.

Seconds later, they were staring into a city of men, women, and children running in panic. Jose and Margie looked around and saw every living thing in it—men and women, young and old, cattle, sheep, and donkeys, being beheaded by the men who were previously marching around the wall.

Margie screamed at Jose: "I can't take it anymore! My mind is exploding!"

Jose screamed back at Margie: "Remember what the rabbit said!"

Blood and body parts were everywhere around them—they could hear a commander in charge say, *"Go into the harlot's house, and from there bring out the woman and all that she has, as you swore to her."*

And the young men who had been spies went in and brought out Rahab, her father, her mother, her brothers, and all that she had. So they brought out all her relatives and left them outside the City. But they burned the city and all that was in it with fire.

Jose and Margie ran along with Rahab and her crew as quickly as they could toward the desert to get away from the chaos of the bloodbath. Although now deep into the desert, they could still hear and see the city burning to the ground. The desert wind was blowing with a harsh sting as Jose and Margie, along with Rahab and her crew, began wandering the desert. They had no clue where they were, or which direction they were headed. In the distance, they could see a dark whirlwind of sand heading their way.

The closer it got, the more violent it became. It was a sandstorm about to consume them. The cyclone then stopped and stood in one spot, swirling like a hula hoop. As the wind whipped and hurled the sand in a circular motion, bodies appeared falling from the turbulent clouds. Without warning, the twister bolted back up into the sky. Jose and Margie ran over to help the fallen sandstorm victims.

Before they reached the bodies lying on the ground, Jose and Margie recognized those features and grumbling voices. It was Skittles, Pits, and Lucas! With only a few minor bumps and bruises from their fall, they were helped to their feet. Ecstatically, they leaped with joy and hugs dominated the moment.

After they finished the celebration, all in one motion, they looked toward Rahab and her crew, as Lucas asked, "Who are all these people?"

Margie told them the story of Rahab, then went on to say all that had happened in the furnace and her other tales. They, in turn, told them similar mind-blowing stories of where they were and what they had been through. Skittles told of being in a tabernacle with candlesticks, lamps, and burnt offerings. Pits spoke of a man who killed his brother, while Lucas watched a man come back from the dead.

Margie put her head down, shaking it back and forth, saying, "I skipped church today, as I do every Sunday. Pits, does your aunt have anything to do with this?"

Pits smiled and said, "Maybe."

Margie was watching Jose and noticed his infatuation with the sky, and she asked what it was that held his attention so vehemently.

Continuing to look up at the sky, Jose blurted out, "The sun's not moving!"

Laughter broke out among them as Margie thought Jose's antics would be followed by some sort of comical gag.

In a more serious voice, Jose said again, "The sun's not moving!"

They laughed it off, until a few hours later when they realized he was right—the sun wasn't moving. Trying not to let Jose's keen observation disturb them, they continued to move deeper into the desert.

Jose was staring at Skittles intently, then began to shout, "Acne! You have acne all over your face!"

Instantly, everyone broke out with the same acne. Gross cherry looking pimples, blistering whiteheads, and creamy blackheads all growing at a rapid rate became dark brown crusty scabs and infected every part of their bodies. Each one had become a hideous looking desert creature. It was so bad that each had to strip naked because the weight of their clothing caused their bodies immense pain.

Now they were all naked, with scabs enlarging to the size of grapefruits. To make things more chaotic, Pits was running around pulling scabs off those unsuspecting innocent strangers traveling with them. Pits only stopped his insane painful actions once Jose did the same to him. Margie told everyone to start picking off their own scabs and save them in baskets.

They painfully did as Margie instructed—collecting twelve baskets full. Days later with hunger pains, they were desperate for food. Their stomachs churned with the thought of those scabs etching down their throats.

Margie said, "Bring the scabs here to me," and she directed all to sit down in the sand.

Taking the scabs and looking up to heaven, she gave thanks and broke the scabs. Then, the scabs turned into bread. She gave the bread to everyone, and *they all ate and were satisfied, and* they *picked up twelve basketfuls of broken pieces that were left over.* Thankful for full bellies, they still had to find their way out of the desert. Margie questioned why she was doing these things, at the same time realizing it was a prompting from within that she knew nothing about.

Meanwhile, Lucas and Jose had different thoughts about which way to go. Although good friends, they were really starting to get on each other's nerves to the point of no longer caring.

Not only did they have different thoughts about which way to go, but Lucas, in his anger, said to Jose, "*If you go to the left, I'll go to the right; if you go to the right, I'll go to the left.*"

Jose's eyes moved back and forth, searching which way he wanted to go. Then, just to annoy Lucas, Jose turned those words in a melody, and started singing, "La-la-la. If you go to the left, I'll go to the right; if you go to the right, I'll go to the left. La-la-la."

In her feeble attempt to defuse the situation, Margie suggested that they try a toe-tapping technique that she would use as a little girl.

Where it came from she did not know—she could only remember the heel tapping, so she began to shout, "There's no place like home! There's no place like home!" while snapping her fingers and tapping her heels. She encouraged everyone to do likewise.

Within minutes, the scenery changed, and they were now performers on stage in a packed colosseum with screaming delirious crowds of people cheering at them. Margie and the Wild Dogs stood alone—absent was Rahab and her crew. They could hear their names being shouted from the crowd, prompting them to perform some sort of spectacular task. They were superstars as adoration and love were being poured out on them—or they thought so.

But they weren't star athletes or great musical performers, but something much greater. They couldn't exactly place a finger on what their status was. Then, with a loud thunder from behind the colosseum walls, slowly appeared a large cage with metal bars rolling toward them. Within the cage was a ferocious roaring lion.

Their fate was to be eaten alive by none other than the Lion of Judah, which Margie had been able to avoid earlier, but it now seemed to be her destiny. Large ropes connected to the bars holding that angry-looking feline captive were pulled from the top of the cage, setting the gigantic cat free.

They were now staring into the eyes of the hungriest, meanest, and beastliest looking creature they had ever seen.

Thinking quickly, Margie began to shout, "There's no place like home! There's no place like home!" while trying to snap her sweaty fingertips and tap her heels, encouraging everyone to do likewise.

Poof! Poof! Poof! Poof! Poof! They were gone! But where to next? Would Margie and the Wild Dogs survive another foot tapping debacle? Could they tip-toe through the tulips? And, away they went!

7
_____

EVERYDAY PIGS

They had regretted that tapping of the shoes because they now found themselves amid a bunch of whining, complaining, agitated people.

And the people cried out to the one in charge with disrespect and loathing, yelling, "*Moses, is it because there are no graves in Egypt that you have taken us away to die in the wilderness? What have you done to us in bringing us out of Egypt? Is not this what we said to you in Egypt: 'Leave us alone that we may serve the Egyptians'? For it would have been better for us to serve the Egyptians than to die in the wilderness.*"

Arguments went back and forth between the leaders and the followers.

Skittles then gathered everyone together in a huddle, saying, "Look, I'm confused here. In the distance, I see an army with horses and chariots coming to kill us all."

Then, Jose said, "The only way out of here is to swim across that sea, which is in front of us."

Margie interrupted the conversation, saying, "The leader of this band of people looks as if he has things under control. Let's wait, look, and listen."

. . .

Then their leader *Moses stretched out his hand over the sea, and the Lord drove the sea back by a strong east wind all night and made the sea dry land, and the waters were divided. And the people went into the midst of the sea on dry ground, the waters being a wall to them on their right hand and on their left. The Army pursued and went in after them into the midst of the sea, all the horses, chariots, and his horsemen. And in the morning a pillar of fire looked down on the Army and threw them into a panic, clogging their chariot wheels so that they drove heavily.*

And the Army commander said, "Let us flee from this people, for the Lord fights for them against us."

Then the Lord said to Moses, "Stretch out your hand over the sea, that the water may come back upon this Army, upon the chariots, and upon the horsemen."

So Moses stretched out his hand over the sea, and the sea returned to its normal course when the morning appeared. And as the Army fled into it, the Lord threw the entire Army into the midst of the sea. The waters returned and covered the chariots and the horsemen; which had followed them into the sea, not one of them remained. But the people and their leader *Moses,* along with their unnoticed guests, *walked on dry ground through the sea, the waters being a wall to them on their right hand and on their left. Thus, the Lord saved the people that day from the hand of the Army.*

Margie and the Wild Dogs looked onto the seashore as the soldiers' mangled bodies washed upon the sand.

Looking to distance themselves from the carnage, they began once again to shout out: "There's no place like home!"

Only now, they were interrupted by the sweet sound of "Hey Margie! Hey Margie!"

After viewing the carnage of bodies washed onto the shoreline, they were now in a land called Leviticus, standing before a high priest named Levi who accused them for the slaughter of the bodies on the shore.

Levi said, "I know we have a law against what you murdering tyrants have done."

Levi searched through stacks of laws that were piled one on top of the other. Margie, Pits, Jose, Lucas, and Skittles stood silently and watched as Levi was determined to file a lawsuit against them.

"Here—here we go," he said as he pulled one of the books off the top of the pile.

Levi opened the book and began to read:

Each of you must respect your mother and father, and you must observe my Sabbaths. I am the Lord your God. Do not turn to idols or make metal gods for yourselves. I am the Lord your God. When you sacrifice a fellowship offering to the Lord, sacrifice it in such a way that it will be accepted on your behalf. It shall be eaten on the day you sacrifice it or on the next day; anything left over until the third day must be burned up. If any of it is eaten on the third day, it is impure and will not be accepted.

Whoever eats it will be held responsible because they have desecrated what is holy to the Lord; they must be cut off from their people.

"Ha!" Levi shouted once he finished before saying, "So, what do you think about that?"

Margie spoke up and said, "Sir, we have not broken any of those laws."

Levi looked at her and said, "Huh, really. Okay, okay. I have others." He reached behind him and grabbed another book from the stack, saying, "I'm sure this book contains your crime."

Levi opened that book and began to read:

If a man sleeps with a female slave who is promised to another man but who has not been ransomed or given her freedom, there must be due punishment. Yet they are not to be put to death, because she had not been freed. The man, however, must bring a ram to the entrance to the tent of meeting for a guilt offering to the Lord. With the ram of the guilt offering the priest is to make atonement for him before the Lord for the sin he has committed, and his sin will be forgiven.

Levi looked at Margie and said, "Did you break one of them?"

"Nope," said Margie.

"Okay, okay, maybe it is one of these?" He continued reading:

When a foreigner resides among you in your land, do not mistreat them. The foreigner residing among you must be treated as your native-born. Love them as yourself, for you were foreigners in Egypt. I am the Lord your God. Do not use dishonest standards when measuring length, weight or quantity. Use honest scales and honest weights, an honest ephah and an honest hin. I am the Lord your God, who brought you out of Egypt. Keep all my decrees and all my laws and follow them. I am the Lord.

As Levi finished reading, he looked up at smiling faces and said, "Huh, I guess not" with a sorrowful look on his face.

Margie then said, "Sir, we are foreigners among you, and you are mistreating us, so you are breaking the law."

"Hum," Levi pouted and said, "I know what to do. I hereby sentence you to the book of Numbers, where you will forever have to count."

They were then banished from the land of Leviticus and taken by boat to the island of Numbers. Upon stepping onto the island, they saw a gigantic welcome sign that read, "Statistics, Population Counts, Tribal and Priestly Figures, and Other Numerical Data." They found themselves before the Numbers leader.

He was a vampire looking man named "Von Count," and he was screaming out, "You will count forever and ever!"

Their sentence was pronounced. Margie, Skittles, Lucas, Jose, and Pits had to count all the people of Israel by families and family groups, listing the name of each man. They *must count every man twenty years old or older who will serve in the army of Israel, and list them by their divisions. One man from each tribe, the leader of his family, will help you. These are the names of the men who will help you: from the tribe of Reuben—Elizur son of Shedeur; from the tribe of Ephraim son of Joseph —Elishama son of Ammihud; from the tribe of Manasseh son of Joseph— Gamaliel son of Pedahzur; from the tribe of Benjamin—Abidan son of Gideoni;—from the tribe of Naphtali—Ahira son of Enan.*

Jose ran off, shouting, "The boredom will kill me!"

The Numbers guards grabbed Jose and tossed him back to the counting crew. The pronouncement was then declared to start. For three months, they counted and counted. *The tribe of Reuben, the first son born to Israel, was counted; all the men twenty years old or older who were able to serve in the army were listed by name with their families and family groups. The tribe of Simeon totaled 59,300 men. The tribe of Gad was counted; all the men twenty years old or older who were able to serve in the army were listed by name with their families and family groups. The tribe of Gad totaled 45,650 men.*

The counting went on, and on, and on before the final calculation. When they were tired and weary, and Margie could no longer take the counting, she begged the Von Count to release them from their sentence. He then made her the offer he thought she couldn't refuse.

He shouted, "Babel. If you can convince God to rebuild the city of Babel, you will be released from your counting duties."

"Convince God? Margie said. Can you give us some idea of what *Babel* is?"

Von Count went on to explain:

Now the whole earth had one language and the same words. And as people migrated from the east, they found a plain in the land of Shinar and settled there. And they said to one another, "Come, let us make bricks, and burn them thoroughly." And they had brick for stone, and bitumen for mortar. Then they said, "Come, let us build ourselves a city and a tower with its top in the heavens, and let us make a name for ourselves, lest we be dispersed over the face of the whole earth." And the Lord came down to see the city and the tower, which the children of man had built. And the Lord said, "Behold, they are one people, and they have all one language, and this is only the beginning of what they will do." So the Lord dispersed them from there over the face of all the earth, and they left off building the city. Therefore its name was called Babel, because there the Lord confused the language of all the earth. And from there the Lord dispersed them over the face of all the earth.

"Wait a minute!" Lucas shouted while looking at Margie. "I want no part of this. We are almost finished counting, so let's just continue!"

Margie agreed, and they continued the final count. *The tribe of Dan totaled 62,700 men. The tribe of Naphtali totaled 53,400 men. Every man of Israel twenty years old or older who was able to serve in the army was counted and listed with his family. The total number of men was 603,550.* The proclamation had finally ended, and with that, Margie and the Wild Dogs were jubilant about their release.

Von Count stood before them, proclaiming, "Good job! My friends, you will now each receive two bags of gold, along with horses and chariots to be on your way."

With that, they jumped with joy—slapping and hip bumping one another.

As the first bag of gold was about to be given to Margie, one of Von Count's minions whispered into his ear: "Psst, psst, psst."

"Now that's an inconvenience," said the Numbers leader as he held back the bag of gold from Margie. "I'm so sorry, but something went wrong with the count, and we now need to do a recount!"

"No! No!" in unison they shouted. "Please, please—we can't do it again!"

Von Count took pity on them, so he gave them two options: do the recount, or go see the Big Dude.

"Who's Big Dude?" They asked.

"He is the leader in the county of Deuteronomy."

Not sure of which option to pick, they agreed to give "the Big Dude" a shot. Behind Von Count's seat was a large doorway that had the words "the Big Dude" written on it. As they entered through the door, they could hear Von Count and his minions snickering beneath their breath. They now stood before the Big Dude, and in one sentence, he declared Margie and the Wild Dogs innocent of all charges.

The Dude went on to say they were in the land of repeats, telling them, "All the charges we would accuse you of have already been dispensed on you back in the land of Leviticus. The door in front of you will set you free of the Pentateuch correction facility, but remember that you are on probation and may return for short periods."

The door they had entered led them onto a perched tower, over-looking a beautiful garden with a scenic view of mountains and valleys. There was no way down, and the door they had come through disappeared just after they entered it. In the distance could be heard galloping steps from what sounded like horse hooves. Sure enough, after several minutes, there stood a knight in shining armor upon his horse.

Looking up, the knight shouted, "Rapunzel, Rapunzel, let down your hair!"

Margie shouted back: "My name is Margie! Not Rapunzel! I'm from the land of the Golden Graveyard! What's your name?"

He answered, "King Solomon." Then, he motioned some dazzling hand jesters before repeating again, "Rapunzel, Rapunzel, let down your hair."

"Okay, okay," Margie said. "What do you want?"

He said, "I will shout up some of my poetry and release the love I hold inside of me toward thou, maiden."

She shouted back down: "My name is Margie! Not maiden! Can you get us down from here?"

"Yes, my maiden, with my poetry."

The Wild Dogs were a bit embarrassed for Margie about the situation but convinced her to play along with him.

"Whatever!" she shouted back as he began to shoot off some poetry.

How beautiful your sandaled feet, O prince's daughter! Your graceful legs are like jewels, the work of an artist's hands. Your navel is a rounded goblet that never lacks blended wine. Your waist is a mound of wheat encircled by lilies. Your breasts are like two fawns, like twin fawns of a gazelle. Your neck is like an ivory tower. Your eyes are the pools of Heshbon by the gate of Bath Rabbim.

Your nose is like the tower of Lebanon looking toward Damascus. Your head crowns you like Mount Carmel. Your hair is like royal tapestry; the king is held captive by its tresses. How beautiful you are and how pleasing, my love, with your delights!

Your stature is like that of the palm, and your breasts like clusters of fruit. I said, "I will climb the palm tree; I will take hold of its

fruit." May your breasts be like clusters of grapes on the vine, the fragrance of your breath like apples—

"Stop, stop! I can't take it anymore! You disgusting pig!" Margie shouted down. Then, she began clicking her heels, saying, "There's no place like home—there's no place like home."

She believed her heel tapping went unheard until she turned around and saw the door re-appear. Without hesitation, they bolted through the door back into the county of Deuteronomy.

Big Dude noticed them right away and shouted, "Welcome back, my friends!"

Then, Margie exclaimed, "We really need another way out of here!"

Big Dude asked them to take a seat while he was finishing up on a court case he had been in the middle of when they popped in.

Big Dude slammed his gavel down and shouted, "Continue!"

Then, the lead lawyer whose name was Geppetto went on to say:

Ananias, together with his wife Sapphira, sold a piece of property.

With his wife's full knowledge, he kept back part of the money for himself, but brought the rest and put it at the apostles' feet.

Then Geptepto said, "Ananias, how is it that Satan has so filled your heart that you have lied to the Holy Spirit and have kept for yourself some of the money you received for the land? Didn't it belong to you before it was sold? And after it was sold, wasn't the money at your disposal? What made you think of doing such a thing? You have not lied just to human beings but to God."

When Ananias heard this, his nose grew very long, and *he fell down and died.* And great fear seized all in the courtroom. Then, guards came forward, wrapped up his body, and carried him out and buried him. Big Dude slammed his gavel and said the court would take a five-minute recess. He then called the group to the bench and asked why they returned.

Margie told the Big Dude that she had been serenaded by a knight with poetry that sounded like a dentist drill.

"Dentist drill?" Big Dude muttered.

Never mind," Margie said, then asked again for another pathway out of the courtroom. "No, Margie." Then, Big Dude looked *at them and said, 'With man this is impossible, but with God all things are possible.* What I can do is change a few things around to rid you of Mr. Poetry."

"That would be fabulous!" Margie replied with relief.

As she finished speaking, the court had started up again. "Order in the court! Order in the court! All rise for Mr. Big Dude!"

Big Dude then asked Geppetto to continue where he had left off.

Geppetto looked and saw the dead man's wife *Sapphira* come into the court, and she had no idea of what had just happened.

Geppetto summoned her to the bench and asked, *"Tell me, Sapphira, is this the price you and Ananias got for the land?"*

"Yes," she said, *"that is the price."*

Geppetto said to her, *"How could you conspire to test the Spirit of the Lord? Listen! The feet of the men who buried your husband are at the door, and they will carry you out also."*

At that moment her nose grew very long, and *she fell down at his feet and died. Then the guards came in, and finding her dead, carried her out and buried her beside her husband.* Concerned their noses would grow like those of *Ananias* and *Sapphira*, Margie and the Wild Dogs bolted back out the Big Dude's door. On the other side of the door, they found themselves standing before an eight-year-old child doing somersaults on a camel leather trampoline, giggling with laughter. Once the child's last bounce bounced, he announced that he was the king of the land. He then ordered them to go to a certain location for a makeover. They were escorted onto a golden chariot, like royalty, to a magnificent castle upon a hill, and their every desire and wish they could imagine would be granted. The largest jacuzzi ever seen was before them, as gigantic bubbles giving off a sweet cinnamon scent awaited them.

The lord and lady of the castle stood ready to scrub down their tired, beat up bodies. The waters were warm and soothing, reassuring them that, at least for the moment, things were good. Flying above the waters of the jacuzzi were tiny cherubim serving them cherries, grapes, melons, chocolates, and the sweetest liquid concoction imaginable. Their taste buds were exploding, sending tingling vibrations shooting from their nostrils, as other cherubim massaged them with soft strokes and gentle pats, sending euphoric sensations throughout their bodies. The pleasure feast ended with a climactic burst of energy that propelled each into separate space capsule chambers.

The capsule holding Margie spun so fast that she lost all consciousness. She woke up to the stench of garbage and was flat on her back. Her eyes were closed, but she could hear snorting sounds ringing in her ears. Afraid to open her eyes for fear of where she was, she just lay still. The snorting continued along with what felt like moisture from a wet rag rubbing against her face. As she slowly gained the courage to open her eyes, standing in front of her was a fat, sweaty, smelly pig.

Pigs were everywhere—hundreds of them—pushing, grunting, squealing, snorting, and farting. She quickly realized that they had landed in a large pig trough. In the distance, she could hear Skittles and Pits calling her name. Coming from the opposite direction, she heard Lucas and Jose shouting but was unable to hear what they were saying.

She knew that something wasn't right when she heard the words, *"If you drive us out, send us into the herd of pigs."*

Margie instantly figured out that her friends were shouting, "Run! Run!"

She could feel herself now part of a wild pig stampede. She was running for her life and trying to keep pace with her pig friends, when she noticed that groups of the pigs were disappearing in front of her. There was a large cliff ahead leading to a streaming river below. Margie was no longer able to keep pace with the piggies, so she jumped onto the back of one of the biggest boars heading toward the cliff. As they were going over the ledge, she could see each Wild Dog riding on the top of his own piggy. Margie's arms and legs were being squashed, beaten, and bullied from the bodies of those out of control swine, and the one thought in her mind was, *Dang! These pigs stink!*

She hit the water with a heavy blunt force, but luckily, she used the pig bodies as her cushion, preventing the impact from killing her instantly. Her pig friends, along with Skittles and Jose, were not so lucky, as she could see their torn, mangled bodies floating down the river. Margie watched as Pits and Lucas climbed safely from the river and headed toward a cave carved into the side of the cliff. Hoping to catch up with them, she moved as quickly as possible toward the cave, but it was too late. They were gone.

8

CHARLIE SAYS

E ntering the darkness of the cave, Margie found herself crawling on her hands and knees in ankle-deep mud. Pits and Lucas were nowhere in sight as she continued her journey. A flash of daylight appeared above her when she realized that her surroundings were the bottom of a well. The only way out of there was back-tracking to the river or shimmying her way up the well's wall.

She began shimmying up the well with her back pressed against one side of the well and her feet and legs pressed firmly onto the other side. Margie had a four-hundred-foot climb, and after ten minutes, she found herself almost to the top. Exhausted from the climb and her feet shaking so badly she was in doubt about making it to the top, Margie started to repeat what had worked for her time and again.

"There's no place like home—there's no place like home."

Her chant was not working, and the next press against the wall found her foot in thick brown slippery mud, causing one foot to slip from the wall. She was now off balance with one leg dangling in the air and her body shaking uncontrollably. She was stuck with nowhere to go but down.

～

Would Margie survive a three-hundred-foot drop? Would all be well in the well? Would it be a case of "All's well that ends well?" Well, we will soon find out!

～

The danger rapidly crossed Margie's mind as she let go and was now in a free fall. She smacked the muddy ground so hard that her body became paralyzed in pain. Stars were floating above her head, and echoes of the crash landing vibrated in her ears. As the sound of bells, whistles, and sirens were ringing in her head, she lay there perfectly still, not wanting to know her physical condition.

A force from above landed on her midsection. It was a thick rope that fell from the top of the well. She heard voices at the top but could not make out what was being said. She rolled on her belly and spread out her arms and legs, praying all her body parts were moving. Although she was in pain and had a pounding headache, she slowly tied the rope around her waist and began her climb to freedom. It took twenty minutes of stop-and-go dangling before she reached the top.

As her hands grasped at the last piece of the well top, someone grabbed her by the shoulders and yanked her out of the well. Margie found herself standing between the well and a middle-aged peasant woman. The woman grabbed onto Margie's shoulders, then shook her so violently that she thought her head was going to snap off. Margie wasn't sure whether the woman was mentally deranged as the woman kept shouting in her face as terrible breath and saliva splashed from her mouth.

The woman kept yelling, "I just spoke to a man who told me everything I ever did! I just spoke to a man who told me everything I ever did!"

"Calm down!" Margie shouted back. "Now, talk slowly, and tell me everything that happened."

The woman began speaking slowly and deliberately:

I came to draw water like I do every day, when this man said to me, *"Will you give me a drink?"* I said to him, *"You are a Jew, and I am a Samaritan woman. How can you ask me for a drink?"* (For Jews do not associate with Samaritans.) He said to me, *"If you knew the gift of God and who it is that asks you for a drink, you would have asked him, and he would have given you living water." "Sir,"* I said, *"you have nothing to draw with, and the well is deep. Where can you get this living water? Are you greater than our father Jacob, who gave us the well and drank from it himself, as also did his sons and his livestock?"* He answered,

"Everyone who drinks this water will be thirsty again, but whoever drinks the water I give them will never thirst.

"Sir, give me this water so that I won't get thirsty and have to keep coming here to draw water." He told me, *"Go, call your husband, and come back." "I have no husband,"* I replied.

Then he said to me, *"You are right when you say you have no husband. The fact is, you have had five husbands, and the man you now have is not your husband. What you have just said is quite true."* I said, *"Sir, I can see that you are a prophet.*

Our ancestors worshiped on this mountain, but you Jews claim that the place where we must worship is in Jerusalem." He replied, *"Believe me, a time is coming when you will worship the Father neither on this mountain nor in Jerusalem. God is Spirit, and his worshipers must worship in Spirit and in truth."* I said,

"I know that Messiah (called Christ) is coming. When he comes, he will explain everything to us." Then he declared, *"I, the one speaking to you—I am he."*

The woman continued, "Then he told me many things no one else could possibly know about me. I then ran into town and told everyone about this man, and now I am telling you!" The woman's grip got tighter as her voice became louder and louder.

Margie managed to break loose from her grip, jump back down into the well, and slide back down the rope. At the bottom of the rope stood two men and a teen. Margie's heart was throbbing as she was glancing at the teen with a noticeable blush, obviously attracted to him. She introduced herself, and in turn, one of the men spoke.

"Hi, my name is Josephus. I am from Jerusalem. My two traveling friends here plucked me from my comforts in Rome, and here I stand."

Margie had a sparkle in her eye as she looked at the teen who was wearing a cowboy outfit, and she asked, "Who are you and where do you come from?"

"My name is Marty from Hill Valley, and my friend here (wearing a blacksmith outfit) is Doc."

Doc went on to explain that they were time travelers who had accidentally landed in Rome in the year of AD 90. Josephus then told Margie that he had been in the middle of writing a historical document when he heard a loud flash, and there appeared before him a chariot holding Marty and Doc.

"Well," Marty perked up and said, "not a chariot, but a mustard yellow Lamborghini."

"What is a Lamborghini?" Margie asked.

"It's a car," Doc said.

Josephus then asked, "What is a car?"

Marty chimed in and said, "Let's forget all that. We need to help Josephus with his historical report."

Josephus explained that back in the early part of the first century lived a man named Jesus, who was an excellent man, who some folks say was prophesied about from a prophet named Isaiah who lived in the eighth century BC.

"My job is to match the life of Jesus with the prophecies from Isaiah."

Doc said that obviously, they had not landed in the correct year and needed to have a do-over. As the four walked deeper into the tunnels, sure enough, they came upon a rigged-up Lamborghini.

Margie spoke up, "I can't believe this! It's a car! It's a car!"

Josephus said to Margie: "Chariot, it's a chariot!"

"Okay, okay," said Doc as he motioned for them to squeeze into the chariot-car.

With the group's arms, legs, and all their body parts twisted and mangled, Doc set the controls for 750 BC to set out to find Isaiah.

"Hey, Doc, you better back up. We don't have enough road in here," Margie said.

Doc stared at her and said, "Roads? Where we're going, we don't need . . . roads."

With a bang and a boom, they found themselves in a courtyard standing next to a man named Marriott, listening to Isaiah hash out prophecies:

Therefore, the Lord himself will give you a sign: the virgin will conceive and give birth to a son and will call him Immanuel. I offered my back to those who beat me, my cheeks to those who pulled out my beard; I did not hide my face from mocking and spitting. A voice of one calling: In the wilderness, prepare the way for the Lord; make straight in the desert a highway for our God.

And the glory of the Lord will be revealed, and all people will see it together. For the mouth of the Lord has spoken.

"Wow! This guy is good," said Josephus. "If I can only hear a little more, I will have my scroll finished."

With that, Doc looked over at Marty and Margie, who were holding hands and whispering to one another.

Doc then said to Josephus, "Okay, a few more minutes, then we need to be out of here. Marty and I have a train to catch."

Josephus looked up and said, "Train?"

Doc just smiled as they continued listening to Isaiah. He was on a rant as prophecy after prophecy left his lips:

See, my servant will act wisely; he will be raised and lifted up and highly exalted. Just as there were many who were appalled at him—his appearance was so disfigured beyond that of any human being and his form marred beyond human likeness. But he was pierced for our transgressions, he was crushed for our iniquities; the punishment that brought us peace was on him, and by his wounds we are healed. We all, like sheep, have gone astray, each of us has turned to our own way, and the Lord has laid on him the iniquity of us all.

"Okay, okay, I have enough!" Josephus shouted. "Let's get out of here!"

The four squeezed back into the Lamborghini and in a flash were gone! Marty was trying to convince Margie to come back to Hill Valley with him before he remembered his girlfriend, Jennifer. Then, in a quick turnaround, the mustard yellow Lamborghini was back in the cave, and with doors opened, Marty gave Margie a swift kick out of the car. She landed in the mud while Doc zapped himself, Marty, and Josephus back to AD 90.

With tears in her eyes, Margie scraped and clawed her way through endless dark tunnels, thinking only of how Marty had just broken her heart. She couldn't see much but sensed human activity around her. At one turn, a trace of daylight crept upon her. She was startled as she found herself watching what she believed was a potential murder in progress. One of several men hiding in the corner of the cave slowly and in deliberate silence approached another man who was naively peeing against the cave wall. The to-be victim was oblivious to the fact he was about to be bludgeoned to death. But, instead of continuing with their plot to murder the victim, one of the men crept up, and as his back was still turned, cut off a corner of his victim's robe. The would-be victim, whose life had just been spared, nonchalantly walked out of the cave.

Monitoring the landscape, Margie could now plainly see hundreds of soldiers who were under the command of that one man. She overheard the predator, who just spared that man's life, say to his friends, *"The Lord forbid that I should do such a thing to my master, the Lord's anointed, or lay my hand on him; for he is the anointed of the Lord."*

Margie watched as the soldiers headed in one direction while their foes headed in the other. Margie turned and headed back into the cave of darkness. She still had no clue where her friends were or which direction to go. Once again, she found herself drenched in darkness, but she sensed she was no longer inside of the cave. Margie was now in absolutely nothing. Nothing above her, nothing below, or around her. She was capsulated where neither time nor space existed. She heard a low hovering sound that got louder and louder while vibrating all around her, followed by the words, "In the beginning."

Margie then had to shield her face from the whitest and brightest light she had ever seen. Following were a procession of events that shook her to the core. She watched as the oceans, stars, the sky, fruit trees, and mountains were created before her eyes. Flocks of birds and every imaginable animal were passing in front of her. What she was watching her lips could not speak, and her mind couldn't comprehend. With a lump in her throat and tears in her eyes, she watched the heavens open, and a White Horse set loose sun sized fireballs that exploded all around her. Everything she had just witnessed that was created moments earlier was obliterated in seconds. She was now in a dust bowl, with only ashes, on top of ashes everywhere.

Margie was covered in soot from head to toe. Embers and dust were still dropping from the sky when Margie saw two cartoon characters appear out of the charcoal dust powder.

They were asking, "Where's Lucy? Where's Lucy?"

Margie asked, "Who's Lucy?"

They went on to explain that they and Lucy had been rehearsing for a theatrical production when the fireballs exploded.

One character said, "One minute, we were in our theater, then the next, we were here."

One character had a bald head, and the other was carrying a blanket.

The kid with the blanket went on to say, "Our creator instilled in me a doctrine."

Margie looked at the bald-headed kid and asked, "What's he talking about?"

He went on to say that once a year, blanket boy would recite certain magical words in their theatrical production that had power and might.

"Could I hear those words?" Margie politely asked.

"I don't know—let me ask him. Linus, can you grant Ms. Margie her wish?"

"Sure, Charlie," Linus answered.

Linus wiped a bunch of dust from his mouth and eyes as he began speaking:

And there were shepherds living out in the fields nearby, keeping watch over their flocks at night. An angel of the Lord appeared to them, and the glory of the Lord shone around them, and they were terrified. But the angel said to them, "Do not be afraid. I bring you good news that will cause great joy for all the people. Today in the town of David a Savior has been born to you; he is the Messiah, the Lord. This will be a sign to you: You will find a baby wrapped in cloth and lying in a manger." Suddenly a great company of the heavenly host appeared with the angel, praising God and saying, "Glory to God in the highest heaven, and on earth peace to those on whom his favor rests."

Before she could reply to Linus' awesome dialogue, those words rung once again in her ears: "Hey Margie! Hey Margie!"

She then found herself between two women bickering about

house chores. The figures in front of her were no longer cartoon characters but real people.

She quietly listened as one of the women shouted, "I'll walk right out that door if you pull that stunt again, Mary!"

The woman being spoken to greeted a company of men at her door.

"Martha, it's good to see you and Mary," said the leader. "Come, ladies, sit while I entertain with deep thoughts about life."

But Martha was distracted by all the preparations that had to be made. She came to him and asked, "Lord, don't you care that my sister has left me to do the work by myself? Tell her to help me!"

"Martha, Martha," the Lord answered, "you are worried and upset about many things, but few things are needed—or indeed only one. Mary has chosen what is better, and it will not be taken away from her."

Martha rolled her eyes while Mary snickered at Martha from under her breath. Not wanting to engage with the scenario, Margie turned her head toward the window, and looking out, saw an old man tying up a young boy over a firepit. In a panic to stop the old man, Margie jumped through the window as the old man reached out his hand and took a knife to kill the boy.

Suddenly, out of the sky, she heard a baritone voice that immobilized her: *"Do not lay a hand on the boy. Do not do anything to him. Now I know that you fear God because you have not withheld from me, your son, your only son."*

Margie watched as the old man untied the boy—then in the same moment grab a ram that was caught by its horns in the thicket and roast it for a meal. The old man noticed Margie staring at him in her statuesque position and invited her to stay for dinner. After she accepted his offer, the old man then introduced himself as Abraham along with his son Isaac. Abraham asked her who she was and where she came from.

She said, "I am Margie from the Golden Graveyard."

She then went on to explain all that had happened to her and the Wild Dogs. She was hoping Abe could give her some insight as to where she was and what was happening to her. Abe went on to explain how he was called out from the land of Ur and headed into a place of the unknown. Abe told her that like him, she was chosen out of the land of the Golden Graveyard, and as with him, she needed to trust God and go with it. Margie then felt a gentle breeze blowing and a warmth in her heart as never before.

Abe said, "You must continue, for you have much to see and learn."

With nowhere to go, Margie asked Abe if she could tag along with him, and his reply was, "Certainly."

As they returned to Abe's cottage, she watched both Abraham and Isaac enter the doorway. When it was her turn to walk into the doorway, a large iron gate slammed the door shut. Then, the large gate immediately lifted again, granting her access to the cottage. Moving forward, Margie took notice that Abraham and Isaac were missing. The room had a fog-like mist, and as the mist began to dissipate, she found herself at a long table with thirteen others.

And their leader at the head of the table spoke, saying:

I have earnestly desired to eat this Passover with you before I suffer. For I tell you I will not eat it until it is fulfilled in the kingdom of God. And he took a cup, and when he had given thanks, he said, "Take this and divide it among yourselves. For I tell you that from now on I will not drink of the fruit of the vine until the kingdom of God comes." And he took bread, and when he had given thanks, he broke it and gave it to them, saying, "This is my body, which is given for you. Do this in remembrance of me." And likewise, the cup after they had eaten, saying, "This cup that is poured out for you is the new covenant in my blood. But behold, the hand of him who betrays me is with me on the table.

For the Son of Man goes as it has been determined, but woe to that man by whom he is betrayed!"

And they began to question one another, which of them it could be who was going to do this.

Margie tapped the guy sitting next to her on the shoulder and said, "Excuse me, sir, please pass me some bread and wine. I'm famished."

The gentlemen passed it to her with a quizzical look on his face. Before he could say the words on his mind to her, a dispute arose among him and the others about which of them was to be regarded as the greatest.

And the leader said to them, *"The kings of the Gentiles exercise lordship over them, and those in authority over them are called benefactors. But not so with you. Rather, let the greatest among you become as the youngest, and the leader as one who serves. For who is the greater, one who reclines at the table or the one who serves? Is it not the one who reclines at the table? But I am among you as the one who serves. You are those who have stayed with me in my trials, and I assign to you, as my Father assigned to me, a kingdom, that you may eat and drink at my table in my kingdom and sit on thrones judging the twelve tribes."*

Margie sensed the leader staring straight at her; then, with a flicker of his eyes, he turned to the guy sitting next to her and said, *"Simon, Simon, behold, Satan demanded to have you, that he might sift you like wheat, but I have prayed for you that your faith may not fail. And when you have turned again, strengthen your brothers."*

Peter said to him, "Lord, I am ready to go with you both to prison and to death."

The leader said, "I tell you, Peter, the rooster will not crow this day until you deny three times that you know me."

And the leader said to them, *"When I sent you out with no money bag or knapsack or sandals, did you lack anything?"*

They said, "Nothing."

He said to them, "But now let the one who has a moneybag take it, and likewise a knapsack. And let the one who has no sword sell his cloak and buy one. For I tell you that this Scripture must be fulfilled in me: 'And he was numbered with the transgressors.' For what is written about me has its fulfillment."

And they said, "Look, Lord, here are two swords."

And he said to them, "It is enough."

They all stood and followed the man in charge as Margie feverishly was tapping Peter on the shoulder, asking, "Who is that man?"

Peter said, "His name is Jesus."

Margie became silent, not able to talk as those words reached her ears.

9

TRUE LOVE

J esus *was walking to a place called the Mount of Olives, and everyone followed him. When he came to the place, he said to them, "Pray that you may not enter into temptation." And he withdrew from them about a stone's throw, and knelt down and prayed, saying, "Father, if you are willing, remove this cup from me. Nevertheless, not my will, but yours, be done."*

And there appeared to him an angel from heaven, strengthening him. And being in agony he prayed more earnestly; and his sweat became like great drops of blood falling to the ground.

And when he rose from prayer, he came to the group and found them sleeping for sorrow, and he said to them, "Why are you sleeping? Rise and pray that you may not enter into temptation."

I wasn't sleeping! Margie was insisting in her mind—because she still could not talk.

While he was still speaking, there came a crowd, and the man called Judas, one of the twelve, was leading them. He drew near to Jesus to kiss him, but Jesus said to him, "Judas, would you betray the Son of Man with a kiss?"

And when those who were around him saw what would follow, they said, "Lord, shall we strike with the sword?" And one of them struck the servant of the high priest and cut off his right ear.

Margie was flabbergasted!

But Jesus said, "No more of this!" And he touched his ear and healed him.

Then Jesus said to the chief priests and officers of the temple and elders, who had come out against him, "Have you come out as against a robber, with swords and clubs? When I was with you day after day in the temple, you did not lay hands on me. But this is your hour and the power of darkness."

Then they seized him and led him away, bringing him into the high priest's house, and Peter and Margie were following at a distance. And when they had kindled a fire in the middle of the courtyard and sat down together, Peter and Margie sat down among them.

Peter said a few words to Margie and noticed that she was not able to speak, and at once said, "I rebuke you evil spirit, come out of her!"

Immediately, Margie began to speak. She was chit-chatting with the girl next to her when the girl looked over at Peter, and looking closely at him, said, "This man also was with him."

But he denied it, saying, "Woman, I do not know him."

And a little later someone else saw him and said, "You also are one of them."

But Peter said, "Man, I am not."

Margie looked at Peter, asking him, "Why are you saying you don't know Jesus?"

He told her, "Quiet!"

And after about an hour still, another insisted, saying, "Certainly this man also was with him, for he too is a Galilean."

But Peter said, "Man, I do not know what you are talking about."

And immediately, while he was still speaking, the rooster crowed. And the Lord turned and looked at Peter. And Peter remembered the saying of the Lord, how he had said to him, "Before the rooster crows today, you will deny me three times." And he went out and wept bitterly.

Margie went outside and tried to console Peter to no avail.

Seconds later with tears in her eyes, she watched as Jesus was beaten. Then in anguish, she witnessed soldiers twisting together a crown of thorns before putting it on his head. Margie was looking to Peter for some answers, but he was frozen in fear. The soldiers continued their assault on Jesus.

They clothed him in a purple robe and went up to him again and again, saying, "Hail, king of the Jews!" And they slapped him in the face as the words "Crucify! Crucify!" floated through the air.

She begged for those words to turn into "Hey Margie," with no such luck. She was then struck with emotional torture as her insides churned with pricking and stabbing pains, as she watched soldiers force Jesus to carry his Cross.

Between Peter and Margie stood a man named Simple Simon who was whispering under his breath, repeating, "No, please not me. No, please not me."

Margie and Peter were pushed aside as the soldiers grabbed and forced Simple Simon to carry the Cross for Jesus. Margie and Peter continued to watch as the soldiers placed the Cross on the ground and held Jesus down on top of it. They nailed His hands and feet to the Cross. The soldiers divided His clothing among themselves by rolling dice to see who would win them.

It was nine o'clock in the morning when they finally crucified him. Above his head, they placed a sign with the inscription of the charge against him, which read, "This is the King of the Jews." Two criminals were also crucified with Jesus, one on each side of him. For three hours, beginning at noon, darkness came over the earth.

About three o'clock, Jesus shouted with a mighty voice, "My God, My God, why have you turned your back on me?" And when Jesus had cried out again in a loud voice, he gave up his spirit. At that moment, the earth shook, the rocks split, and all went dark.

Margie then found herself within the darkness bouncing on a waterbed. What she heard next captured her attention. Two voices, one conversation.

One voice was asking, *"From where have you come?"*

The other answered, *"From going to and from on the earth, and from walking up and down on it."*

And the first voice said to the second, *"Have you considered my servant Job, that there is none like him on the earth, a blameless and upright man, who fears God and turns away from evil?"*

Then, the second voice answered, *"Does Job fear God for no reason? Have you not put a hedge around him and his house and all that he has, on every side? You have blessed the work of his hands, and his possessions have increased in the land. But stretch out your hand and destroy all that he has, and he will curse you to your face."*

And the first voice said to the second voice, *"Behold, all that he has is in your hand. Only do not kill him."*

Margie bounced off the waterbed and followed the second voice to a house in which a party was occurring. From a distance, she watched as a powerful wind swept in from the outskirts and struck the four corners of the house. It collapsed on all the people inside, killing everyone. Or so, that is what Margie believed at the moment. From under the rubble, she could hear faint moaning and groaning.

Running toward the sounds, she began lifting some of the rubble, and to her amazement, two bodies crawled out. She was astonished to see it was Lucas and Pits. More sounds from a few feet away sent her to remove more rubble with two more bodies appearing—it was Jose and Skittles. They were bruised and battered but conscious, and just a little feeble.

"How did you get here?" Margie asked them.

They answered in unison, "The pigs brought us here!"

Pits went on to say that the family whose house was just destroyed had invited them in, but they quickly enforced the "no pigs in the house" rule. But the pigs were fed and tended to generously outside. Skittles joined in to say that the morning before, a lightning bolt came from the sky and killed all the pigs. So, there they were in the house having a big pig dinner with the family when the house was struck by lightning and collapsed.

"Margie!" Skittles said, "Are you paying attention to me?"

"No," she said as her focus was on watching the sky open.

From above, they heard shouts of *"Clean, unclean, clean, unclean,"* while at the same time, *a large sheet* was *being let down to earth by its four corners. It contained all kinds of four-footed animals, as well as reptiles and birds.*

"Hey, look!" Margie shouted. They gasped, approaching the humongous bed sheet with curiosity.

As they drew closer, they were being sucked onto the sheet unaware, like a fly stuck on flypaper. The more they struggled to escape, the tighter the sheet held them in place. Then in reverse, the unfolded sheet began folding back up into the sky with everyone aboard. As they were being coiled up like a roll of toilet paper, Margie and the Wild Dogs, along with every animal, bird, and reptile, were being squeezed so tightly that their heads began popping off—their crushed bodies full of blood were being poured out from the sheet like Kool-Aid. Margie's mangled, bloody body was sucked off the sheet. She now found herself in sound body and mind on the inside of a gigantic room, being pushed down onto a soft cushioned seat resembling an emperor's throne.

Next to her, on his own cushioned throne, sat a vibrant, spunky middle-aged man, wearing yellow clothes, a red and white striped shirt, yellow gloves, and clown shoes with yellow laces.

He was smiling profoundly at Margie, and her reaction was a timid smile back, as she said, "Hi, I'm Margie from the Golden Grave-yard," to which his response was, "Hi, I'm Ronald from Kroc County."

They both spoke at the same time, saying, "Why are you—"

Then, each stopped and said, "You first" to one another five times before Margie screamed, "Stop it!"

He became quiet, and Margie asked in a low tone, "Why are we here?"

"I don't know why you're here, Margie," Ronald answered. "From me, He wants big results."

"Results? What results?" Margie asked.

"I've been commanded to put ten of His writings onto small rocks, then put them into a red cardboard box with a yellow smiley face on it and call it the 'Happy Box.'"

He held up the Happy Box and shook it to his ear. Rattling inside were the ten stones, clacking together.

"What are the writings on the stones?" Margie asked.

Ronald pulled one rock from the Happy Box at a time, reading each one out loud.

You shall have no other gods before Me.
You shall not make idols.
You shall not take the name of the LORD your God in vain.
Remember the Sabbath day to keep it holy.
Honor your father and your mother.
You shall not murder.
You shall not commit adultery.
You shall not steal.
You shall not bear false witness against your neighbor.
You shall not covet.

When he had finished the readings, he gently placed each rock into its own little private box, calling them his pet rocks. Margie realized he had been in that room for an exhausting period.

Then, as if she were possessed, a voice came spewing from her mouth that said, "You deserve a break today, so get up and get away."

Ronald was then crushed like hamburger meat from a heavy metal hydraulic and pushed deep into his cushioned throne as Margie was clamped tightly onto her throne with heavy leather straps.

10

A DAY IN BIFF'S LIFE

Margie sat strapped alone for hours, in a quiet, somber state of mind, not able to comprehend consciousness. Then, in one gravitational swoop, all of her mind and body sensors returned, and she was released from the leather straps. Her eyes then focused upon a led doorway with the words inscribed upon it: "Stairway to Heaven," and portrayed below it was the emblem of a blimp. Standing at the doorway, Margie knocked, and answering was a one-eyed creature.

It said to her, "Now—what do you want?"

"I want to see Him," said Margie.

The creature snapped back at her, "Not nobody! Not no how!"

"But I'm Margie from the Golden Graveyard—"

"Margie from the Golden Graveyard? Oh, you are. Well, bust my buttons! Why didn't you say that in the first place? That's a horse of a different color! Come on in!" said the creature. "Just wait here—I'll announce you at once."

Margie was exhilarant, repeating the creature's words: "He'll announce me at once!" "I've got as good some answers now," Margie blurted out as she danced to a happy dance, whirling her arms and legs in circles.

The creature returned moments later and said to Margie: "Go on home! He says to go away!" Then, the creature rudely slammed the door shut.

"Go away?" Margie muttered? "Oh no!" Margie then began crying uncontrollably. Under a stream of tears, she said, "Oh—and I was so happy! I thought I was getting answers."

Peeking from behind the door, the creature had sympathy for Margie and said, "Oh, oh—please don't cry anymore, little lady. I'll get you in to see Him, somehow. Come on in, Margie."

As she entered, a voice louder than a trumpet said, "Come up here, and I will tell you why you are here and what is to be done next."

With one step forward, she was before God's throne. Her eyes were then peeled backward into her head—it was now her mind's vision that interpreted all of God.

The one sitting on the throne was as brilliant as gemstones—like jasper and carnelian. And the glow of an emerald circled his throne like a rainbow. Around the throne were twenty-four thrones, and seated on the thrones were twenty-four old men, clothed in white garments, with golden crowns on their heads. From the throne came flashes of lightning, and rumblings and peals of thunder, and before the throne were burning seven torches of fire, which looked like seven spirits of God, and before the throne there was as it were a sea of glass, like crystal. And around the throne, on each side of the throne, were four living creatures, full of eyes in front and behind: the first living creature looked like a lion, the second living creature like an ox, the third living creature with the face of a man, and the fourth living creature like an eagle in flight.

And the four living creatures, each of them with six wings, were full of eyes all around and within, and day and night they never stopped saying, "Holy, holy, holy, is the Lord God Almighty, who was and is to come!"

And whenever the living creatures gave glory and honor and thanks to him who was seated on the throne, the twenty-four older men wearing the crowns fell down before him who was seated on the throne and worship him.

They cast their crowns before the throne, saying, "Worthy are you, our

Lord and God, to receive glory and honor and power, for you created all things, and by your will, they existed and were created."

Margie sat with her head down, frozen in unbelief—staring down at the floor as her eyeballs receded back to the front of her head, full of tears.

Then, an authoritative, strong voice said," Hey, Margie! Come now!"

Margie bowed down and stood staring at the floor before *Almighty God*.

Then He spoke saying, "Margie, I love you. I have loved you before the beginning of time. This adventure you have been on was a snapshot of your father's life. Biff was a good man *after my heart."*

Stuttering profoundly, Margie squeaked, "My father?"

"Yes, your father. We had a bond, he and I—we loved each other. But he found another love, one with other gods."

"I don't understand," Margie said.

"Now, please stay silent, and I will explain. It was before your birth that your father and I had become good friends. He loved me. *But I have this against* him*, that* he *has abandoned the love we had at first.* Biff was young, juvenile, and arrogant when he and I solidified our bond. That Sunday morning would be no different than any other for Biff. He woke up and got out of bed, combed his hair, then made his way downstairs. While enjoying his cereal and juice, he noticed he was late. Biff grabbed his coat and hat and made it out the door in seconds. He was so proud of his Harley Davidson motorcycle that he had purchased only one week earlier with those hard-earned paychecks.

"He rode to the meeting place, where he, Stan, Buzz, Chains, and Foghorn discussed their childhood dream. That dream was to ride South into the sunset, free as birds, and with the carelessness of a raging fire. Not one of them had yet reached their nineteenth birthday before pledging that oath of brotherhood. Three days later, they found themselves down South in an out-of-control house party. Drugs, alcohol, and women were the care of the night.

"Biff's reckless entanglement that night caused havoc throughout the house, sending him in handcuffs to the county jail. This jail had only weeks before granted permission to a local church to establish a ministry within their walls. The church known as 'the Summit' had a small group of men who would go into the facility each Sunday, with guitars in hand, lead a worship and praise segment, then a sermon with mentoring to the inmates afterward. Biff not only stayed in his cell as the Sunday service was conducted, but he bad-mouthed it continually—until one Sunday when he heard a catchphrase that he had not heard in years. That phrase came from Porky. Porky was one of the volunteers who served the inmates each Sunday. His name was a nickname, not because of his weight or lifestyle, but because he had that famous tagline from the cartoon character Porky Pig: 'Th-th-th-that's all folks!' Porky had that line down perfectly and would make the inmates laugh whenever he shouted it out.

"It just so happened that Biff was a secret Porky Pig fan. As a young boy, Biff practiced that tagline for years, never quite perfecting it. So, Biff and Porky quickly bonded a friendship off that tagline. Each Sunday, when Porky showed up, Biff would run from his cell, shouting the tagline 'Th-th-th-that's all folks!' waiting for Porky's reaction. Porky was a blessed clever evangelist for the Lord, and through his Porky Pig voice was able to present the gospel to Biff in a way he had never imagined. Biff had told Porky that he always believed to be a follower of Christ, one had to act and dress a certain way. He told Porky his idea of a Jesus follower was someone who skipped down the road with flowers, acting in a peculiar manner.

"One night, after Porky had left, Biff devoured my Word. He stayed up many hours that night pouring out his heart and surren-dering to me, asking that I be his Lord and Savior. I could not deny such a heart-wrenching request. The next Sunday, Biff couldn't wait for Porky to appear and tell him the exciting news. When Biff spotted Porky, he grabbed his cellmate by the collar and dragged him to Porky.

'Tell him, tell him!' Biff excitedly exclaimed!

"His cellmate, whose name was Daffy, looked at Porky, with a big smile on his face then proclaimed in a quacking voice, 'Woo-hoo!

Woo-hoo! Woo-hoo! Biff led me to the Lord last night, and I have accepted *Jesus as my Savior!*'

"With that great news, the guitars began to ring out, as a celebration to the Lord prompted others to follow in Daffy and Biff's footsteps. Your father's relationship with the Lord was tested daily, as loneliness and fatigue set in. Every day, he was on his knees begging Me to have him released from that jail cell. He was a completely broken young man, and I was his only friend, outside of Porky. Our relationship was solid, and he would sing, pray, and meditate on Me. My Word became a basket full of joy in his life, as he would sit and read, hour after hour, and story after story. When he came upon these words, his heart gave way, and he accepted them as his own:

Be strong and very courageous. Be careful to obey all the law my servant Moses gave you; do not turn from it to the right or to the left, that you may be successful wherever you go. Keep this Book of the Law always on your lips; meditate on it day and night, so that you may be careful to do everything written in it. Then you will be prosperous and successful. Have I not commanded you?

Be strong and courageous. Do not be afraid; do not be discouraged, for the Lord, your God will be with you wherever you go.

"Those words brought your father tremendous faith, as he believed each word. Then, he cried out loud as he read the words that I had spoken while visiting earth: '*Come to me, all you who are weary and burdened, and I will give you rest. Take my yoke upon you and learn from me, for I am gentle and humble in heart, and you will find rest for your souls. For my yoke is easy, and my burden is light.*'

"He was so sincere, having hopes and dreams. Then, that dreaded night came when I granted his request, and he was released from jail. I remember that night every day.

"'Twas the night before Christmas, when all through the jail, not a creature was stirring, not even a snail. The stockings were hung by the bars with care—in hopes that St. Nicholas soon would be there. The inmates were nestled all snug in their beds, while visions of sugar plums danced in their heads.

"On that beautiful night, Biff grieved the *Holy Spirit, with whom* he *was sealed for the day of redemption.* Two correction officers, Mr. Teddy and Mr. Behr, walked into his cell, telling him to pack his belongings and that he was being released. The expression on his face told the whole story. He became smug and prideful, puffed up, proud, and he had that sinister look in his eyes, which I had not seen since the day he was incarcerated. His release process took three hours. The only thing he possessed as a free man was the Bible he so dearly treasured. As he was about to walk out of jail, he swore never to return. The last things Biff saw walking out of jail that night were three large bins. The first bin had the word 'garbage' written on it, the second bin had the word 'recyclables,' and the third bin had a mocking handwritten sign that read 'the Bible Shredder.' Your father quickly examined the three bins.

"Holding the Bible close to his heart, he fought his conscience not to toss his Bible into the Bible Shredder. To his credit, and a quick prayer, he was able to overcome that temptation. He walked out of the door with a sigh of relief and comfort with his newly acquired freedom. But little did he know that only a few feet outside the door waiting were his biker buddies, Stan, Buzz, Chains, and Foghorn. He was startled as he walked out to cheers and harmless mocking from his brotherhood. The harmless mocking included the words 'Jesus Freak,' which sent Biff into a panic. With a quick mumbling excuse, he turned back swiftly into the building. He said a hasty 'I'm sorry' prayer, then tossed his once precious Bible into the bin displaying 'the Bible Shredder.'

"The moment his Bible hit those blades, life for your dad would never be the same—it was an earthquake of monumental significance, a deep sinkhole of catastrophic proportions. His life was now trapped in the snares of the evil one, going from one lie to the next. That Bible was given to him by Chaplain Dumas. During your father's incarceration, he not only promised Me he would change his ways but also made that promise to the chaplain."

Margie was intrigued by what she was hearing and leaned in a bit closer.

God continued, "That Bible so flippantly tossed into the bin was ripped into shreds and buried at a local landfill. What you, Margie, have been experiencing was your father's life inside that shredded Bible. You have seen only parts of My story with jumbled sequences of my love. You have experienced what occurs when the secular world and spiritual world collide—when My attributes become mixed and blended. Not knowing fantasy from reality. Never understanding the true meaning behind the word 'lukewarm.'

"Your father's life has since been full of fear, guilt, and panic, although you would not know it because he hides it well. Biff is not alone in shredding My Word. It happens every day, as believers come to Me in distressed times, seeking My help. Many plead and beg for My mercy in troubled times. Yes, I am a God of mercy and love, but I *will not be mocked* with broken promises. I hear time and again how I am the All in All in a believer's life, until good times return. Then, I am put on a shelf, like an old, forgotten toy. Many homes have two, three, even four Bibles sitting idle. Those who do not read them are as far from Me as that shredded Bible in the local landfill. My Word is life—it is more essential than food and water. Those who search Scripture find Me. Many shred their Bibles in the doings of this world—searching for happiness in wealth, health, comfort, and ease. When a person wakes, My Word should be the first thought on their mind, not breakfast. Without the Word, there would be no breakfast. Is it possible to leave home without Me? No, I am there. Trips to and from school and work would be so much more delightful on a belly full of Scripture.

"When your father neglected me, I watched, and it was not entertaining to see the anger, bitterness, rage, and fury build up against imaginary foes, the evil one projected into his mind. He had no defense; I just watched and waited for his call, which never came. At the workplace, more are concerned about lunchtime than about Me.

Yes, I hurt at these times. Those who talk to Me continuously are blessed with My friendship; those who know Me because of Scripture have a certain way about them.

"Margie, I sent My Son to explain all these things in person. Still, those who are Mine struggle with simple faith. My Word began when I opened my mouth, creating the universe and all in it. What I ask of you, Margie, is that you share your experiences with your dad—let him know I still love him. He will understand. Do this quickly!"

11

THERE'S NO PLACE LIKE HOME

Margie's eyes were then shut as she heard voices shouting, "Hey Margie! Hey Margie!"

Opening her eyes, she saw hovering over her Travon, Skittles, Lucas, and Jose. Margie was lying flat on her back, looking up and wondering once again where she was. Travon beganto speak, "Margie, we thought you were dead! How you survived that fall off the wall is incredible!"

"Wall? What wall?"

As Margie sat up, she remembered her adventures inside the shredded Bible. *But was it a dream?* she asked herself. They told her that they last saw her on the top of the wall in her Supergirl position, and each apologized for the rock-throwing incident that caused her to rush and fall from the wall. She asked them how long she had been passed out.

Skittles said, "It took us thirty minutes to break through the wall, and we have been trying to wake you for ten minutes now."

"I must get home! I must get home!" Margie began shouting.

"Margie, relax!" Lucas said, as he held her hand, trying to comfort her.

"You don't understand—it's my dad! I must see my dad!"

As she was getting to her feet, she looked down on the ground, and to her disbelief, there was Dad's shredded Bible and a dead rabbit. The Book was held together by the binder with duct tape. The pages were torn and mangled. The rabbit was crushed to death when she fell on top of it from the wall top. Although they had not understood the significance of the Book, the rabbit, or Margie's unstable character, they got her home as quickly as possible.

As they arrived home, the Wild Dogs stood outside while Margie stormed toward the house. She saw her dad in the pigeon coop feeding the Dobermans and raced over, ignoring the fact that once again, she was about to be pounced on by the canines. The Dobermans knocked her to the ground once again, licking and snuggling up against her body as she shouted for them to stop. Her dad ran from the pigeon coop, ordered the dogs away, and helped his daughter off the ground, giving her a big loving hug and asking why she looked as if she'd been through a grinder. Her answer was that she believed she had been. Then, she showed her dad the shredded Bible. Biff took it from her and examined it while flipping through the torn pages.

"What is this?" he asked. They could hear her mom Peggy yelling from the house, asking if everything was okay.

"Yes," Biff answered as his eyes jolted back and forth from Margie to the shredded Bible. "I don't understand, Margie. Where did you get this?"

She went on to explain all that had happened to her and that she had believed it was all a dream until she found the Bible.

"Is it true? Did you toss the Bible into the shredder?"

With tears in his eyes, Biff walked Margie into the coop and asked her to sit, telling her, "I have a lot to explain, and it's not nice."

Then, he began to speak, "It's true—all true. When I was in jail, the best advice I received was not to go back to those bad influences in my life, which at the time were Stan, Buzz, Chains, and Foghorn. If they just hadn't been waiting for me outside the jail that night, everything would be different. I caved in, Margie, I caved! Things are bad— very bad. Your mom wants a divorce, and the police are about to arrest me any day now. We are going to lose our house, and your brothers are addicted to drugs."

Margie stood silently listening as her dad continued, "I knew that day as I tossed the Bible that God was real. He spoke to me, Margie; He spoke to me! I became a fool! I tried to juggle Him and this world. I compromised and rationalized everything to be His will for our family. I believed He gave me the power to make wise worldly decisions. I trusted Him when I should have been *following* Him."

By this time, Biff was crying like a baby with tears flowing from his eyes. "I don't know what to do! God has shared my life with you; I am so embarrassed and exposed—to my baby girl. How can I make things right?"

While falling to his knees, he then said, "What do I need to do, Margie?"

With tears streaming from her eyes, Margie was feeling her dad's pain both physically and emotionally. She reached over and took the shredded Bible from his hands, and scuffling through it, came to this Bible verse: *"Forget the former things; do not dwell on the past. See, I am doing a new thing! Now it springs up; do you not perceive it? I am making a way in the wilderness and streams in the wasteland."*

Margie began to tap her heels and repeat the words *Jesus Christ, Jesus Christ, Jesus Christ.* Margie's eyes began to roll into the back of her head as she fell to the ground having a seizure. Biff screamed for help, shouting for Peggy to call 911. The Wild Dogs, who had been patiently waiting outside, heard the confusion and came running to the coop, helping Biff carry Margie into the house. Margie was rushed to the local hospital by ambulance where she lay in a coma for days.

Vigils were held and church services conducted as mighty prayer warriors prayed for Margie's life. As Biff sat by his baby's bedside weeping, he listened to those around him in gentle voices sing "Amazing Grace."

Then, a tiny voice spoke into his ear, saying, *"Relax, everything's going to be all right; rest, everything's coming together; open your heart— love is on the way!"*

With those words, Margie's eyes slowly opened, and she could hear soft whispers of "Hey Margie!" as her fuzziness of mind subsided. Standing before her stood Mom, Dad, Dave and Duncan, the Wild Dogs, the Skittle sisters Mary and Elizabeth, and Mr. Gabriel, all circled around her hospital bed.

Unaware of her condition, she smiled at her dad, saying, "It worked—it really worked."

"Yes, HE did," Biff answered. "How are you feeling, Margie?"

"Thankful, very thankful." She asked everyone to hold hands, and with tears flowing down her face, she prayed, *"Our Father in heaven, hallowed be your name. Your kingdom come, your will be done, on earth as it is in heaven. Give us this day our daily bread, and forgive us our debts, as we also have forgiven our debtors. And lead us not into temptation but deliver us from evil. Amen."*

When Margie had finished praying, she and her dad gave a loving wink to one another, and in unison, said, "Th-th-th-that's all, folks!" *And they lived Happily Ever After.*

EPILOGUE

Margie went on to adopt three words from her experience within the wall of the Golden Graveyard that would give her life blessings. Biff and Peggy lived in a beautiful, loving home. Her brothers Dave and Duncan went on to lead holy and exalted lives. The Wild Dogs all amplified spiritual, divine lives, all trusting *Jesus as their Savior*. Margie found her Prince Charming, and together, they had three beautiful children, along with three beautiful grandchildren, all who glorified and worshipped God, doing many great things to help move *His Kingdom* forward.

These are those special words Margie carried for a lifetime:
"IF GOD WANTS."

Note from the Author: Margie and the Wild Dogs have a special request to the awesome readers—if you could please leave a review for this book on Amazon, that would be fantastic!